MELTING MATILDA

THE GRANITE EARL AND THE ICE MAIDEN

JUDE KNIGHT

I'm dedicating this novella to the sister writers who were with me through the steps of creating it, the Bluestocking Belles. You'll see their characters working with mine on a charity event at the Frost Fair on the Thames. It was a winter that brought London and the rest of England to a grinding halt, and that killed those who couldn't get out of the cold, including veterans of the Napoleonic wars and the orphans and widows of those who serve. We based our box set around raising money to make a difference.

Thank you to Caroline Warfield for loaning me some of your secondary characters from your novella: Lady Georgiana Hayden, the Marquess of Glenaire, the Earl of Chadbourn.

Sherry Ewing, thank you for Lady Constance Whittle, and two of the friends of your hero, Lord Digby Osgood, (James Marr and Vernon Mellbarrow).

Rue Allyn, I enjoyed including your Percy Cummins as close friends with my Jessica. Thank you for her and Trevor, Lord Trehallow.

MELTING MATILDA

Can the Ice Maiden soften the Granite Earl?

Her scandalous birth prevents Matilda Grenford from being fully acceptable to Society, even though she has been a ward of the Duchess of Haverford since she was a few weeks old. Matilda does not expect to be wooed by a worthy gentleman. The only man who has ever interested her gave her an outrageous kiss a year ago and has avoided her ever since.

Can the Granite Earl melt the Ice Maiden?

Charles, the Earl of Hamner, is honour bound to ignore his attraction to Matilda Grenford. She is an innocent and a lady, and in every way worthy of his respect—but she is base-born. His ancestors would rise screaming from their graves if he made her his countess. But he cannot forget the kiss they once shared.

Melting Matilda was first published as a novella in the Bluestocking Belles' collection *Fire & Frost*.

1

If the two of them made it out of the near-invisible city streets alive, Matilda Grenford was going to kill her sister Jessica, and even their guardian and mentor, the Duchess of Haverford, wouldn't blame her. Angry as Matilda was, and panicked, too, as she tried to find a known landmark in the enveloping fog, she couldn't resist a wry smile at the thought. Aunt Eleanor was the kindest person in the world, and expected everyone else to be as forgiving and generous as she was herself. Matilda could just imagine the conversation.

"Now, my dear, I want you to think about what other choices you might have made." The duchess had said precisely those words uncounted times in the more than twenty years Matilda had been her ward.

When she was younger, she would burst out in an impassioned defence of whatever action had brought her before Her Grace for a reprimand. "Jessica is not just destroying her own reputation, Aunt Eleanor. Meeting men in the garden at balls, going out riding without her groom, dancing too close. Her behaviour reflects on us all."

Was that the lamppost by the corner of the square? No; a few steps more showed yet another paved street with houses looming in the fog on both sides. Matilda stopped while she tried to decide if any of them were in any way familiar.

Meanwhile, she continued her imaginary rant to the duchess. "Even in company, she takes flirtation to the edge of what is proper. This latest start — sneaking out of the house without a chaperone or even her maid — if it becomes known, she'll go down in ruin, and take me and Frances with her."

Matilda had gone after her, of course, taking a footman, but she'd lost the poor man several mistaken turns back. Matilda had been hurrying ahead, ignoring the footman's complaints, thinking only about bringing Jessica back before she got into worse trouble than ever before. Now Matilda was just as much at risk, and she'd settle for managing to bring her own self home to Haverford House, or even to the house of a friend, if she could find one.

Home, for preference. Turning up anywhere else, unaccompanied, would start the very scandal Matilda had followed her sister to avoid. If Jessica managed to make it home unscathed, Matilda would strangle her.

In her imagination, she could hear Aunt Eleanor, calm as ever. "Murder is so final, Matilda. Surely it would have been better to try something else, first. What could you have done?"

Matilda startled herself with a bark of laughter that echoed oddly in the fog.

"Why did you not tell me, or your nurse?" Aunt Eleanor had asked a thousand times, when Matilda had found herself in hot water because she had tried to pull Jessica from trouble of the girl's own making. She could never explain; not without hurting Aunt Eleanor's feelings.

Jessica had been her best friend since they were babies in the nursery, nearly as close as twins though they had different mothers. She and Jessica — part of the Grenford family, but only by Her Grace's charity — belonged to one another and didn't quite fit anywhere else. They were a family of two. They finished one another's sentences, dried one another's tears, and kept one another's secrets. Their half-sister Frances, the youngest of Her Grace's wards, was separated by a gap of years from their magic circle.

Matilda began walking again, alone in the fog. Surely, if she kept to streets of the houses of the wealthy, she might at last come to a place she knew? She crept along the paved footway, seeing the houses loom one by one out of the gloom into sharper detail then sink away behind her into oblivion again. The sun was somewhere above the fog. At least, she supposed it was still shining, and strongly enough to illuminate a small space around her, as if the fog grew thinner wherever she moved.

Perhaps it was the same with her and Jessica. They had been separated by the fog of Society's expectations, and could no longer clearly see the love that had shone between them for their entire lives, since Jessica was a few days old and Matilda not quite six months.

From the time they came out in the Season of 1812, they had grown apart, as those around them accepted suitors, married, and started families of their own. No one wanted wives of dubious origins, even if they had been wards of the Duchess of Haverford since infancy, and would be well dowered by the marquis, her son. Matilda tried harder and harder to be a pattern-card of ladylike behaviour, while Jessica took more and more risks.

Now, they each moved in their own little circle of fog, but they still kept one another's secrets, and that was why Matilda had not confided her worries to the Duchess of Haverford, or even to her guardian's son, the Marquis of Aldridge.

Today's escapade was beyond enough. She must tell Aldridge. If she made it home safely, she would unburden herself to him.

She swallowed a little — not from fear, exactly. She was not afraid of the marquis: source of presents, occasional donor of curricle rides, stern protector against gentlemen who could not be trusted to behave with respect. Awe was a better word than fear. Aldridge might be the Merry Marquis to the rest of the world, but to the sisters, he was more proper than the most rigid maiden aunt.

She thought of the power of his raised eyebrow, which had more than once warned her and her sisters from stepping outside the boundaries of acceptable behaviour. Of course. Aldridge could save Jessica from herself. Matilda should have talked to him before.

Having dealt with the future to her satisfaction, she stopped on another anonymous street corner to face the present. Was that the sound of someone walking towards her? Yes, surely. Smothered by the fog, but coming closer. Should she call out? Hide?

She longed for rescue. She feared attack, or even discovery, which would be a longer drawn-out agony but quite bad enough. Torn with indecision, she stood as if her boots had become frozen to the paving slabs.

Charles Stapleton, Earl of Hamner, could have been alone in London. Fog muffled sound as well as sight, so that his boots and his walking stick rang out their cadence in a little bubble of clarity bounded by half-seen shapes and half-heard noises.

Every sixty or seventy paces, he came to another oil lamp, left alight long after dawn since even the lamplighters might get lost in the gloom. He counted doorsteps and corners to find his way, and welcomed each new lamp that confirmed his position, though its dim light failed to do more than illuminate the moisture in the air so he moved from halo to darkness and back to halo again.

On the very edge of visibility, a formless shape resolved into the silhouette of a person, standing just within the penumbra of a lamp. As he drew closer, it became clear she was a lady, or at least dressed like one. What was a lady doing alone in the streets on a day like this? On any day, of course, but especially in such gloom.

Charles lifted his hat in greeting, and sensed rather than saw her shoulder's ease. Did she think an assailant unable to ape good manners? Stride by stride he approached, and stride by stride she came into better focus.

His heart sank as he recognised her. Of all the females to need his help, it had to be the Haverford Ice Princess. Nonetheless, manners demanded that he lift his hat again, bowing. A slight bow, peer to commoner, but still a bow. He fiercely resented the necessity, telling himself that a female with her breeding — or lack thereof — should not expect such recognition from a gentleman, but the ward of the Duchess of Haverford had every right to be treated with respect.

Miss Grenford returned a small curtsey, though a quick darting look at the fog hinted that she no more wanted to be rescued by him than he wanted to play knight errant to her.

Matilda Grenford had been bedevilling Charles since she first made her entry to Society, side by side with her equally problematic sister. No. She was more problematic.

"Lord Hamner." Just that, and in freezing tones. No explanation of her presence alone in the street. No pleas to see to her safety. No smile.

"Miss Grenford." How he wished Miss Grenford were more like her sister so he could blame her, instead of himself, for the insult that had sunk him so low in her regard. He'd fought an unwelcome and inappropriate lust in her presence since he asked her to dance at her debut ball two years ago. It was, of course, only lust. He would have recovered long ago, he was certain, if she had been in his keeping, but that would never happen.

Besides, for all that he told himself he would tire of her, he could not imagine it. He would not take a mistress he could not give up. He had sworn on his mother's grave that he would have no other women when he married. He would never do to his wife and children what his father had done; marrying a proper lady when his heart was with his irregular family.

To marry Miss Grenford was unthinkable. When he wed, it would be to a maiden of pure bloodlines, both maternal and paternal. He owed it to his name. He owed it to the heir he and his wife would raise to the dignities of his title, and to any other offspring.

To offer protection to a ward of the Duchess of Haverford was impossible. She behaved like a proper lady, whatever her appearance. If he compromised her, he would be honour bound to offer for her, and would do so without even the incentive of an angry brother. The Marquis of Aldridge would avenge insult to any of the Grenford sisters, and Aldridge was deadly with both sword and pistol, but Charles's own sense of what was due a lady would propel him to the altar without such a threat.

Sometimes, he struggled to remember that would be a bad outcome. If only she were more like her sister.

Miss Jessica Grenford appeared a proper Society maiden, but she skirted the edge of propriety and would soon fall over it, just as one might expect from someone with her family history. Miss Matilda, on the other hand, looked like every man's dream of the perfect courtesan, from the dark curls that framed her lovely face to the lush form that the most demure gowns ever made for a Season could not disguise.

The most optimistic of rakes could find nothing of the *demi-monde* in her speech or behaviour. One wag had suggested that the 'ice' of her nickname was the sweet confection for which Gunthers was famous, but it was a lie. She was cold, and all the efforts of the cleverest flirts, the most lyrical poets, and the most ardent charmers could not strike a spark to heat her above freezing.

Only Charles had seen a glimpse of the vibrant passionate woman within, on one occasion that remained memorable no matter how hard he tried to forget it.

His lust—and it must be lust, for he would not allow it to be anything more—was doomed to remain unrequited. Even if some less honourable cur compromised her and failed to give her the protection of his name, the duchess was unlikely to cast her off. The woman had an unaccountable habit of offering refuge to fallen women, and would surely extend such help to her own ward.

"May I escort you home, Miss Grenford?" Charles asked. "To Haverford House," he added, lest she mistook his intentions.

Stiffly, she accepted his offered arm. They took a pace or two into the fog before she spoke.

"I must thank you, my lord," she said, her voice redolent with barely subdued resentment. "My footman and I were separated in the fog, and then I lost my way. I despaired of finding my home again."

Sympathy with her predicament warred with irritation at her tone, however much he might deserve her contempt. It was not his place to scold her, but he could not resist. "You should not have been walking in this at all. The fog hasn't lifted in days, so you cannot have thought it safe to be wandering around the streets, without so much as a footman to protect you from nuisance."

He could barely see the beautiful face turned up to his, but the wave of anger at his presumption was palpable. Her voice was chillier than ever. "I am obliged to you for correcting my faults, Lord Hamner."

She attempted to withdraw the hand that clutched his arm, but he refused to allow it, covering it with his own. "Tolerate my arm for a short while longer, Miss Grenford, lest we become separated in the fog."

Her reluctant hand was a brand on his arm, setting fire to his whole body. He should have let her leave his side and would have, had not the danger of the fog been very real.

Their silent march had brought them to the gates of Haverford House. "This way," Miss Grenford said, stopping by a little side gate, that let onto the side of the large entry courtyard.

She released his arm. "Thank you, Lord Hamner," she said again. "I do not know what..."

They were interrupted as the gate opened, and a woman darted out, her mouth already moving. "Oh, miss. You're safely home. I was that worried, miss." She danced around her mistress, patting one arm, brushing off the back of the cloak, poking a finger at the reticule.

Behind her came a footman, who also ignored Charles as if he did not exist. "My lady, I'm that sorry. I thought you'd be here ahead of me, and then you weren't and I was going to go back out and look for you. But my lord said I'd only get lost again, and then..."

She was interrupted by a firm, "Enough, Beckham." The marquis had followed the two servants through the gateway. "Your lady is here, Marsh, and she is safe," he told the maid. Now off you go and make sure she has water to wash and a nice cup of hot chocolate to warm her."

Aldridge smiled at Matilda before turning to Charles with his hand extended. "Thank you for seeing my sister safely home. As you can see, she lost her footman in the fog."

"She should not have been out in the fog," Charles grumbled. He had more to say, but a look from Aldridge stopped him.

The marquis's response was quiet, almost contemplative. "I do not permit others to rebuke my sister, Hamner, however grateful I might be for her rescue."

Charles could do nothing but accept the set down. However much Miss Grenford needed to be reined in, he had no right to argue about it with Aldridge, who was ten years his senior. He was acting head of the ducal family, besides, with the old duke suffering the final consequences of decades of dissipation.

"I will take my leave, then," he said, his bow just a shade on the correct side of perfunctory.

"Will you not come in for a drink before you brave the fog again?" Aldridge asked.

"Thank you, but no. Navigating in this weather means every trip takes twice as long as it should, and I am already late."

"I am sorry to have taken you out of your way," Miss Grenford said, polite if reluctant.

Charles bowed again. "I shall hope to see you in more clement weather, Miss Grenford, Aldridge."

He was nearly out of sight in the fog, but not out of earshot, when he heard the lady say, "Aldridge, Jessica is out..."

The marquis interrupted her. "Shush, Tilda. Not out here. Everyone is safely inside. Let's get you in, too."

So, it was as Charles thought. Miss Grenford was once again putting herself at risk to save her reckless sister.

2

Matilda couldn't bring herself to betray Jessica. She couldn't deny that she'd gone out after her sister, for which she received a gentle scold, but she didn't tell Aldridge about the other occasions and about her fears.

She would make one more attempt to reason with Jessie, she told herself, to justify assuring Aldridge that everything was fine; that he needn't worry. If Jessie wouldn't promise to stop taking such terrible risks, then Matilda would tell Aldridge.

He frowned down at her. When did he develop those fine networks of worry lines in the corners of his eyes? She put up a thumb and tried to flatten them out. "Truly, Aldridge. You have enough to concern you."

"I will always have time to be concerned about my sisters, sweet Tilda," he assured her, the pet name making her feel even more guilty about her deceit. He changed the subject. "Did Hamner bother you?"

"No more than usual," Matilda said. Aldridge's face hardened, and she realized what he meant.

"He is always such a prig," she added. "He dared scold me as if I were a thoughtless child. He has no right."

Aldridge offered his arm and escorted her to the door of the family wing, where he left her to return to his own quarters. She hurried upstairs. She expected Jessica to be waiting for her in their private sitting room. She did not expect to be attacked as soon as she walked in the door.

"How could you set Aldridge onto me?"

"I did nothing of the sort. I will though, if you won't promise me to be more careful, to stay home, to stay safe. Jessie, anything could have happened to you out there."

"I was perfectly safe. You should just trust me. Instead, you take off after me, and then you let your footman come back first and tell Aldridge that we are both missing."

"I didn't *let* the footman come back," Matilda protested. "I lost him in the fog. I thought you were lost too. I certainly was. If Lord Hamner had not been the one to find me… Please, Jessie, won't you tell me what is going on?"

Jessica turned to look out the window, hiding her face. "I can't, Tilda, and you mustn't ask me. Just trust me."

It was other people Matilda didn't trust, and the physical yearnings that Jess, too, must surely have inherited from her own mother. Matilda had kept the secret of her own reaction to Lord Hamner and his devastating kiss; could she really insist on knowing Jessica's secret? "I do. I just worry. Jessie, if people find out…"

Jess spun back around, her eyes widening in alarm. "People mustn't find out. Tilda, it is not my secret, and I am doing nothing wrong. Don't ask me questions. Don't follow me. I promise I will be careful, and when I can, I will tell you all about it." She flopped down into one of their fireside chairs, somehow making the unlady-like drop look graceful. "Now, tell me about the Granite Earl. Did he really rescue you?"

"I suppose he did." Matilda giggled as she remembered Lord Hamner's face. "He was very unhappy about it too. Dear gracious, the man deserves his moniker. He does not unbend even a little."

His arm felt like granite, too, under her gloved hand. It wasn't just that he had once kissed her. Something in her—and what could it be but her mother's blood—had thrilled to the touch of him since the day they first met two years ago, in the early days of her first

Season. Why it should be Hamner and none other, she had no idea, but it was so.

Perhaps it was fortunate he had treated her from the first with a distant courtesy edged around by disapproval. On the one occasion he did not—if he had not stopped, and backed away stammering, she might not have stopped him. Heaven alone knew how far her low appetites might have led her astray.

Instead, she avoided him. When she couldn't, she met his strained politeness with her own frosted civility.

Jessica rose to her feet. "We had best change for the meeting, Tilda. The Society for Brats is coming."

Oh, yes. One of the duchess's charities was meeting here today, rather than in the Oxford Street bookshop and tearooms that was their usual meeting place. *The Ladies' Society for the Care of the Widows and Orphans of Fallen Heroes and the Children of Wounded Veterans* intended to hold a fundraising event in a few weeks, when most of the ton had arrived in London. Even the dreadful fog could not be allowed to interfere with deciding what that event was to be.

The maid they shared brought them warm water to wash, and they helped one another into afternoon gowns suitable for receiving company.

"This is my third change today," Jessica commented. "Yours too, I take it."

Matilda knew what was coming. She and Jessica had been deputed to the duchess's causes since they were old enough to help, but for some reason this one had got right under Jessica's skin, and just last week, she had all but accused their benefactor of hypocrisy.

Jessica ignored her silence, repeating the essence of what she had said to the duchess. "The cost of the gowns we have already worn today alone would have provided a year's care for one of the indigent families for whom we were fundraising."

Matilda gave her the answer that Her Grace had given last week. "If we both dressed in sackcloth, Jessie, it would still be not enough. Aunt Eleanor says that we need to draw money out of those who would not otherwise give. To do that, we need to be seen as part of the *ton*, and that means we need to dress the part."

Jessica was not convinced. "If Aldridge would give me my dress allowance, instead of paying my bills, I could get by with half the clothes I have. I know I could."

They dropped the conversation as they entered one of the less formal parlours, where the duchess waited for them, her current companion at her side, and Cedrica Fournier, her previous companion, already seated before a table, pen and paper ready to take notes.

Madame Fournier had left her position to marry, but she had volunteered to be secretary for this committee. Jessica and Matilda took turns in greeting her with a kiss in the vicinity of her cheek, and as they did, the other ladies began to arrive.

The first part of the meeting was given over to reports. The work of the Society was organised by small groups, sometimes as few as two or three ladies. Lady Felicity Belvoir, through her connections to half the families of the *ton*, kept them aware of social events at which they could canvas for votes in Parliament. Lady Georgiana Hayden was in charge of writing pamphlets to sway opinion, and Lady Constance Whittles marshalled a miniature army of letter writers for the same purpose.

Many of the Society's members also volunteered at hospitals where injured veterans were nursed and orphanages that cared for veterans' children. They visited widows where they lived, some in very insalubrious areas. The duchess agreed with the necessity; how else were they to meet real needs if they did not first talk to those who were suffering? She insisted on the volunteers and visitors travelling in groups and being escorted by stout footmen.

Once all the groups had reported back, they discussed their next fundraising event. The ladies offered one idea after another. The duchess would hold a charity ball, of course, as she did every year, but none of them felt that would be enough to really draw attention to the cause. Something special was called for. Something unusual.

Matilda was not sure who suggested a Venetian Breakfast, but the star suggestion of the day came from a shy girl who was new to the Society. Miss Fairley rose to her feet and waited for Mrs. Berrisford, the meeting's chair, to notice her.

"I wondered if we might hold a picnic basket auction," she said, flushing pink at being the centre of attention. We have done them at home as fundraisers for the church, and they are very popular."

Two of the ladies objected that midwinter was hardly time for a picnic, but Mrs. Berrisford called for silence. "Go on, Miss Fairley," she encouraged. "How does it work?"

"The ladies provide a basket of food," Miss Fairley explained, "and the gentlemen bid for the right to share the basket with the provider. It is usually the single ladies, of course." Her voice faded almost to nothing as her blush deepened to scarlet.

Mrs. Berrisford called for order again, as the Society's members all tried to express an opinion at once.

The duchess rose, and those who had not already stopped talking fell silent to see what she thought. "If we can ensure propriety, ladies, such an auction would be just the thing to bring in donations from the younger gentlemen, who are far more likely to spend their funds on less helpful activities."

That settled it, of course. Discussion turned to ways and means, and before the meeting was over, several more groups had been established, to cover the various aspects of three events: Venetian Breakfast, auction, and ball, all on the same day.

"Could the auction prize include a dance at the ball later?" Jessica made the suggestion. "That way, gentlemen who have bought a basket will also be obliged to buy a ball ticket."

The suggestion was met with a hum of approval.

"We will need to enlist the ladies of the ton," Mrs Berrisford said. "I suggest each of us talks to as many as possible; older ladies to the mothers, younger to the girls. The men, too, of course; but ladies first."

"We can start at Lady Parkinson's in two days' time," one of the other ladies proposed.

That seemed to be the end of the decision making, though many of the members lingered for another cup of tea and one of the delicious little cakes Monsieur Fournier supplied to the duchess for her meetings.

Matilda and Jessica, in their role as daughters of the house, moved from group to excited group, knowing Her Grace would wish to know what was being said in these more casual conversations.

Everyone was excited by the plans, and more than one person was hoping that the fog would lift so that Lady Parkinson's soiree would proceed and they could begin their campaign.

Charles had promised to escort his mother to the evening event with which Lady Parkinson intended to start the Season, some two weeks ahead of anyone else. They would only go, he insisted, if the weather allowed.

To his private dismay, the morning of the event dawned clear, with no fog. Charles pointed out that the heavy clouds presaged snow, but his mother declared she was starving for a sight of her friends and a little bit of company, and she would not be staying in tonight unless the snow was actually falling.

"We will leave Lady Parkinson's if the snow starts," Charles insisted. He would rather not go at all. Two Seasons ago he had set his sights on a bride, and around this time last year, his courtship had been roundly rejected. He'd managed to avoid most of last year's Season, but meeting Lady Felicity Belvoir had not become less awkward on the few occasions they met. She was in town again; he knew that. Would she be there tonight?

He consoled himself that Lady Parkinson had called it a "small evening gathering of close friends, with perhaps a little dancing for the young people", but she had misrepresented the event. Over two hundred people were jammed into the lady's string of reception rooms. It seemed that everyone who had come early to London was of the same mind as Lady Hamner, desperate to leave their own homes.

Charles escorted his mother through the rooms until they found her friends.

"Now run along, dear, and find someone to dance with."

Did he ever enjoy this kind of event? It wasn't fashionable for men to admit to any kind of pleasure in a ballroom, but two years ago, this would have been a treat. He would not have sat out a dance though; nor would he have danced twice with the same female.

He loved the company of women, from the innocent pleasures of dancing and conversation with Society's maidens to the more robust and earthy delights to be savoured with discreet widows.

A wealthy earl needed to be cautious. but if he went nowhere alone, and paid attention to them all and not to anyone in particular, he raised no expectations and could simply enjoy himself. He had. Until he met Miss Grenford. No! It wasn't that. His downfall was setting his sights on Lady Felicity.

There she was now, in conversation with the duchess's two wards. For the last two seasons, Miss Grenford, Miss Jessica, and Lady Felicity had been close friends. After the duchess's house party last Christmas, the lady's older sister had married and almost immediately gone into mourning for her husband's grandfather. Rather than miss the Season, Lady Felicity had been taken under the duchess's wing. The three young ladies clearly intended to spend this Season together, as they had the last.

It was intolerable that he wanted to yearn after Lady Felicity, who would have made him a perfectly unobjectionable wife: an ornament to the Hamner name. Instead, he could barely look at her. Not when she stood next to Miss Grenford.

As he continued around the room, he fought to control his reaction to the pernicious female's presence. He was not the only one. He heard her name, and slowed to listen.

"Miss Grenford is the living image of Angel," sighed Lord Amhurst. The elderly earl, recently elevated to the peerage in his brother's shoes, was leering at Miss Grenford and her sister. The old lecher was talking to his new young wife's brother, Basil Driscoll, and two of his other drinking companions

"What a woman Angel was," said one of the others. "Do you remember back when Winshire's cub George nearly got shot by Haverford for singing love songs outside her bed chamber window, accompanied by a small orchestra?"

"Should have chosen another night," Lord Amhurst chuckled. "Haverford did not appreciate being disturbed while swiving."

Charles had heard such stories before. Angel Kelly had brightened their disreputable youths like a shooting star. Warm-hearted and merry, she traded one lover for another till she reached the zenith of the courtesan's profession with a duke for a protector, and not just any duke, but the Duke of Haverford. Angel then disappeared, and a short while later, Matilda, the first of the Grenford wards, turned up in the keeping of the duchess.

Lord Amhurst sighed. "If ever a girl was born to follow in her mother's footsteps… I mean, just look at her."

What a disgusting comment. Miss Grenford was not her mother. She was a walking incitement to lust, but that was hardly her fault. She was also a properly behaved lady, who had never — to his knowledge — by word or act given the rakehells cause to hope for her fall. Even that kiss—it was the innocence in her response that had finally penetrated his mad desire enough to allow him to wrench himself away.

One of the other old lechers shook his head. "Want my opinion, the Duchess has ruined her. Born to be a mistress; raised to be a wife. She will never find a place to fit in."

"It's disgusting," Amhurst agreed. "Foisting the spawn of a woman like that on decent people."

"It's the sister we should be watching, Amhurst," remarked Basil Driscoll. "That one is ripe for the picking. It's only a matter of time until she falls into some lucky bastard's hands. So to speak." He smirked. "If she hasn't already. What else was she doing in Berkley Street in Clerkenwell a few days ago, all on her own, coming out of one of the houses?"

"Did you ask her?" The man who asked the question was leering, and signalling his opinion of the encounter with both eyebrows.

"I lost her in the fog, but I think we can all guess what she was up to. Exactly what I want to do with her when I get her alone."

Charles was sorely tempted to smear Driscoll's lascivious grin from one side of his smug countenance to the other, but the Grenford sisters did not need the scandal of having men fight over them. Instead, he went hunting for Miss Grenford. He needed to grit his teeth and petition her for a dance, despite how the lady's touch stoked his inappropriate response to her. It was the only safe way to find the privacy to warn her about the rumours.

3

Matilda stared in shock at the elegant figure before her. If the Granite Earl was imposing in his daytime wear, he was enthralling when dressed for the evening, all in black but for his white cravat and gloves, and his embroidered silver waistcoat.

"Miss Grenford?" He was too polite ever to sound impatient, but his imperious hand hinted that he expected an answer, and assumed it would be affirmative.

Jessica gave her a nudge. If Matilda did not accept Lord Hamner's invitation to dance, she would be unable to accept any others this evening, and then Aunt Eleanor would wish to know why. She managed to smile and curtsey.

"Thank you, my lord." She placed her hand in his, and even though they were both gloved, his touch set her quaking. Heaven's mercy! It was a waltz: an entire set dancing with him alone, holding his hand, his arm around her, staring into his eyes. Why had he asked her to dance?

No one she had danced with since she came out—whether bored, charming, slyly lecherous, condescending, pompous, or openly eager to court the favour of Her Grace or Aldridge through her—no one affected her like Lord Hamner.

She had felt it the first time they danced, a week or so into her first Season, nearly two years ago. A tingle when they touched. An awareness of his physical presence even when they were separated by the patterns of the dance. An aching response in her own body, as if she were suddenly hollowed out and yearning for something unknown.

He did not ask her again that Season, though they frequently attended the same events.

The next time was at the Masquerade Ball held at the duchess's Christmas house party at Christmas that same year. When she accepted his invitation, she hoped that her previous response reflected her inexperience. But all the dances in between, all the partners in between, made no difference. If anything, the sensations were worse.

He felt something, too, she was sure, because he became stiffer than ever, and would barely look at her. When the music ended, he held his arm away from his body and escorted her to the nearest side of the floor. Noticing how flushed she was, he suggested some fresh air, but as soon as they were alone, the proper distance between them vanished. He kissed her. She kissed him back, her heart singing, only to drop through her dancing slippers when he walked away. She repulsed him with her wanton response: she just knew it.

He left the party the next day, but that was nothing to do with Matilda. Lady Felicity, but her friends called her Fliss, told those closest to her that he had proposed—and Fliss had refused him–the very next morning after that magic kiss, the rat. If Matilda hadn't known he thought her only fit for dalliance, that news would have confirmed it.

He'd been missing for the first months of last Season, and transformed into the Granite Earl by the time he first put in an appearance. Now, he seldom graced a Society ballroom, and even less frequently a dance floor.

They took their positions, with their nearest arms along one another's shoulders, their other arms clasped in front of them. Four march steps, and they changed, Hamner grasping Matilda's right hand with his behind her back, as she put her left hand in his. She could feel the warmth of his arm against her back.

Dear Merciful Goodness. How would she ever bear an entire waltz? If last time's occasional touches had been bad, the amplified response this time threatened to destroy her. What had been a tingle was now sharp enough to be almost painful, except that it was somehow pleasurable, too, coursing through her body from the points at which they touched to the lower parts of her torso one would never speak of or even think about.

Barely aware of her actions, following the cue of the music, she faced him and offered him her right hand. He lifted it for the pirouette and they turned slowly, their hands resting on one another's waists.

Her insides ached until she feared she would lose the contents of her stomach. She was so hot, she thought she might melt, and wouldn't that cause a sensation? Matilda Grenford, smeared across the dance floor in a puddle of desire.

She was nearly two years wiser than when she first met Hamner. Still an innocent, in every sense that mattered to Society, but not so naive as to be unable to name the feelings he aroused in her so easily, while he—unspeakably annoying man—showed nothing but his granite mask.

"Miss Grenford?" He had been speaking, and she hadn't heard a word.

"I beg your pardon, Lord Hamner." How very rude she was being.

He was polite enough not to roll his eyes, but both expression and tone were so bland as to hint at his irritation. "I asked for this dance, Miss Grenford, so I could warn you."

Her eyes opened wide, and —for the first time since the waltz began — she fully met his gaze. "Warn me of what?" she asked.

"You must be very careful. Your sister, too. Especially your sister. I don't like to repeat what I've heard, Miss Grenford, but you must be careful to go nowhere alone or with a gentleman."

What did he mean to imply? "Are you performing this public service for all the young women here tonight, Lord Hamner? Lady Felicity, for example?"

That cracked the stone façade. He lifted his chin, and a light flush stained his cheeks. "I am not concerned about Lady Felicity, Miss Grenford."

Of course not. Fliss was legitimate and a Belvoir, of impeccable lineage on both sides. "I see," she replied, turning her head deliberately so she was not looking at him.

"Miss Grenford, you misunderstand." Lord Hamner didn't miss a beat in the dance, gliding to one side so that her right arm pressed against his chest, and his crossed her torso under her breasts. The effort not to melt into his arms made her snappy.

"Do I misunderstand, Lord Hamner? Do you not intend to imply that women of our scandalous heritage cannot survive the smallest and most innocent misdemeanour?"

"Just listen to what I say," he growled, his voice strained.

That, and the superior scorching look, set a match to her temper. "I do not answer to you for my behaviour; nor does my sister. I will thank you to keep your opinions to yourself. You are not my keeper."

He had been reaching for her hands again, having dropped them as he moved to take her back into the first waltz position. She drew out of reach as her words brought him to a halt.

"Someone needs to be your keeper," he snapped. "Your brother has no control over you, it seems."

Had she really used the word 'keeper' with all that it implied? Burning, she turned her embarrassment into outrage. "You pompous prig. How dare you."

"Devil take it! Keep your voice down. Come. I'll escort you back to Her Grace." Lord Hamner offered her an arm.

Conscious of their fascinated audience, Matilda forced her mask of unconcern back into place. She put two fingers on Lord Hamner's arm and allowed him to escort her from the dance floor, being careful to stay as far from his side as she could.

The duchess hurried to meet them; her eyebrows raised in question. "Aunt Eleanor—" Matilda took a deep shuddering breath, determined not to further entertain the assembly by releasing the tears that threatened.

Aunt Eleanor, her eyes sharp as she examined first Matilda and then Lord Hamner, took both Matilda's hands and hers. "My poor dear. Is it one of your dreadful headaches again? My thanks, Hamner, for bringing her to me. She needs a darkened room, and no noise. I will take her home."

With her arm around Matilda's shoulders, the duchess began shifting towards the door, sending those around her on errands: one to make her apologies to Lady Parkinson, another to fetch Jessie, a third to send for the Haverford carriage.

Hamner was given his own mission. "Find Aldridge, Hamner, if you would be so good, and explain to him exactly what has happened."

Matilda was swept along, with nothing to do but retain what dignity remained to her by refusing to succumb to her tears. Consumed in her own struggle, perhaps she was only imagined the hint of a scold in Aunt Eleanor's voice when she dismissed Hamner with his own errand.

Charles obediently set off to look for the duchess's son. Thank all the powers that be for the great lady's social skills. She had taken the disaster he had made of his attempt to warn Miss Grenford, and defused any possible scandal from their altercation on the floor, provided no one heard the lady insult him. No. Her tone might have been clear to those dancing nearby, but not the actual words.

The supposed headache was a convincing excuse for Miss Grenford's pallor, the strain around her eyes that hinted at incipient tears, the way she wilted against the duchess. Charles had done that, with his ill-chosen words. If Aldridge called him out for it, it would be no more than he deserved.

Aldridge met him before he'd completed his circuit of the first room.

"Hamner, a word," the marquis said. He was in full ducal mode; no hint of the charm with which he usually masked his formidable nature. Charles followed him out into the entry hall, which was as crowded as the reception rooms. After one glance at the mob, Aldridge led the way up the stairs, and then past the card room and the withdrawing room where more party goers clustered. With an autocratic wave, he passed a footman stationed to protect the private parts of the house, and opened the first door beyond, into a private sitting room clearly furnished for the lady of the house.

"I'll have an explanation for that scene on the dance floor," he said, his voice arid.

Charles swallowed. "First, I have a message from Her Grace." Best carry out that commission while he was still in one piece. "She has taken Miss Grenford and Miss Jessica home. Miss Grenford was unwell. A severe headache."

"Taken unwell suddenly while waltzing with you, Hamner. What occurred to bring on this 'severe headache'?"

"I meant—" Charles swallowed again. "I meant only to warn her to be careful, my lord. I overheard a conversation..." How to put this? Already, he had insulted Miss Grenford without meaning to do so. Insulting her and Miss Jessica again, and this time to the dangerous man who called them his sisters, would be foolish in the extreme.

Aldridge narrowed his eyes, perusing Charles's face, then his own face relaxed, the familiar hints of humour lighting his eyes. He crossed to a row of decanters on the other side of the room, and filled a couple of glasses. "Brandy," he explained as he handed one to Hamner. "Lady Parkinson has an affection for it, though she would prefer that fact not be widely known."

He waved to a chair and sat down himself, completely at ease with appropriating the lady's private room and her decanters. "I have always thought you a decent sort, Hamner, even when you were on His Grace's leash. Indeed, your good character is the reason you no longer bark to his command." Charles made no comment, merely nodding in acknowledgement of the restrained compliment. He had, indeed, been the Duke of Haverford's disciple until he was forced to realise that the man was completely without honour.

"That being the case, I shall give you five minutes to explain the reasons you felt urged to 'warn' my sister. You have a tendency to be pompous, but I have seen no evidence that you are crude or immoral. Or, at least, not more immoral than the rest of us."

The term 'pompous' hurt, especially since Miss Grenford had

used the same words. Still, Aldridge was in the right. Charles laid out exactly what had happened, from the overheard conversation to exactly what was said during the waltz.

A couple of judicious questions later, he found himself recalling as much as he could of the walk in the fog, and even what he'd heard of Miss Jessica venturing where she shouldn't, and his own observations of Miss Grenford putting herself at risk to keep her sister safe.

The five minutes was long gone when Aldridge allowed him to fall silent. He sat and sipped his brandy while the marquis stared into nothing. Finally, the man gave a single nod.

"I will have your word you will say nothing of what I am about to tell you to either of my sisters, Hamner. You have shown an admirable concern for them, and you have earned the right to know. Besides, I have no wish for your uninformed concern to drive Jess, in particular, to defy me by practicing the very behaviour we are trying to avoid."

Charles inclined his head in agreement, saying, "You have my word, Aldridge."

"I have men following both of my sisters at all times. I am aware that their invidious position makes them vulnerable, and my own commitments mean I cannot always be in place to warn off those unwise enough to think I would not protect my own." His lips curved in a smile that looked more like a threat.

"Had you been anything less than a gentleman that day in the fog, my friend, you would have met one or more of those guardians."

The smile vanished. "I am pleased to be alerted to young Driscoll's interest. I shall deal with it, I assure you. Next time you hear anything of the sort, bring the information to me or—in my absence—to my secretary, Edmund Markinson, who is fully in my confidence."

He stood, and Charles put down his empty glass as he got to his own feet.

"Shall we?" Aldridge waved towards the door. "Oh. And Hamner? Two more things. First, you should know that one of my first duties once I am Duke of Haverford will be to publicly acknowledge all three of my sisters as daughters of the previous Duke of Haverford."

Charles blinked at that. The recognition would make a difference with most, if not with the highest sticklers. In one stroke, the duchess's orphaned wards would become acknowledged connections to the might and power of the House of Haverford; accepted sisters of its head.

Aldridge had followed his thoughts. "Yes, precisely. Given the state of His Grace's health, my sisters' days on the fringes of the marriage mart are certainly numbered, though in my eyes, their actual status will not change. They are very dear to me."

Charles knew that to be true. While the Duke of Haverford ignored the existence of his wife's wards, and would certainly have denied being their father had anyone had the temerity to make the accusation in his presence, the duchess and her sons treated them as if they were legitimately the daughters of the house. Nor was their paternity in any serious doubt. The youngest, still in the schoolroom, was a female version of her father. The eldest was clearly the daughter of a woman the duke had in his keeping at the time the child was conceived. The whole world assumed the middle one was from the same stable.

"The second thing?" Charles prompted.

Aldridge wrinkled his brow in question.

"You said 'two more things'."

Aldridge regarded him steadily until Charles had to fight not to shift as uncomfortably as a truant schoolboy under the eyes of his tutor. "I think that one thing is enough for today, Hamner," he said at last. "Shall we return downstairs?"

Charles followed him from the room. He'd survived the encounter with nothing more than a mild scold. Further, Aldridge had favoured him with a couple of confidences. He could avoid Miss Grenford and her sister with an easy conscience. Why, then, did the thought of doing so fill him with dismay?

4

Matilda came down to breakfast, heavy headed after a night of confounding a dream version of Hamner with one witty and devastating retort after another. Between each victory, she slipped into an uneasy sleep, only to wake restless and aching with the fleeting remnants of a dream in which she and Hamner waltzed again, sometimes in a crowd and sometimes alone, but always with his touch opening yearning possibilities within her.

Aldridge was before her at the table. Since he lived in the heir's wing, on the other side of the mansion's massive public rooms from this, the family wing, his presence was unusual. Matilda wished she had taken a tray in her room, or waited for Jessica, or perhaps run away to Spain, now nearly free of the French, to join a convent.

Anything to avoid an inquisition on her early departure from the soiree.

The marquis stood to greet her. "Good morning."

Matilda dipped a curtsy, and took the chair he held for her. One of the footmen poured her coffee, and another fetched her a soft bread roll, all that she felt she could eat this morning.

"That will be all for the present," Aldridge told the servants. "Wait in the hall, if you please."

Matilda put down the piece of roll she had been about to eat, her mouth dry. "I'm sorry I made a fuss. Was it very bad?"

Aldridge put his hand over hers and smiled. "Everyone accepted you were taken ill with a sudden headache, Tilda sweetheart. I am not here to scold you. Hamner took complete responsibility for the whole incident."

Even as she breathed a sigh of relief, Matilda fought the urge to deny Hamner the right to full responsibility. How dare he explain things to her brother? Pompous, arrogant, self-righteous man.

"Is that what you came over to tell me?" she asked.

"That, and to assure you that I am looking after our Jessie. You and Hamner don't need to worry. I will handle it. Trust me, Tilda?"

"Hamner? Worried?" Unladylike though it was, she snorted at the thought. "Hamner is worried about his own consequence."

From the twist of his lips, Aldridge was amused. "He is accounted charming by some. You might ask yourself why he is so stiff with you."

Matilda was well aware of the reason for that. "He disapproves of my entire existence."

Aldridge's smile broadened.

"He does, Aldridge, and it is not funny."

Aldridge shook his head. "He is certainly different in your presence than he is in the company of anyone else, including Jessica." He said nothing more, addressing himself to the last few items on his plate.

Matilda knew this trick of his. She was not going to be the one to speak first. She took a sip of her coffee, followed by a piece of bread roll. Aldridge seemed to be implying that Hamner had an interest in her. It was ridiculous. Hamner would never court the daughter of an Irish harlot, and he was far too righteous to insult the sister of a peer with the other kind of offer.

Aldridge had followed his breakfast with a tankard of light ale, and Matilda had finished her own repast before the silence was broken by Jessica. She entered the breakfast room followed by the servants who had been waiting in the hall.

"Am I interrupting anything?" she asked.

Aldridge held the chair on the other side of Matilda, and

pushed it in as Jessica sat. He leaned over and gave each of the sisters a kiss on the cheek. "Have a pleasant day," he said. "It's snowing quite heavily, so take that into account when you're making your plans."

He left without saying anything more.

Jessica finished giving her breakfast order to a footman. "What did Aldridge want?" she asked Matilda.

Matilda had to tell her something. For Aldridge to join them for breakfast and then to send the footmen out of the room required explanation. "I will tell you later," she promised.

When they got back up to their sitting room Matilda was able to content Jessica by saying Aldridge wanted to discuss the incident at Lady Parkinson's. Of course, Jessica also wanted to know why Matilda had been so upset but 'Hamner was rude' was enough to stop her questions, and they settled down to make a joint list of names of the ladies they had spoken to the previous evening about the coming fundraising event.

Over the next few days, the snow proved to exceed Aldridge's worst prophecies, making evening engagements impossible, and daytime outings perilous. The two sisters were deputed to one of their least favourite activities: writing endless letters to men and women of influence, alerting them to the conditions facing the families of those injured or killed while protecting Britain against the aspirations of the Corsican.

A slight thaw came as a relief—one compounded for Jess when her friend Miss Cummins came to stay. A scandal had driven Miss Cummins into hiding, but Aunt Eleanor intended to see her re-established in Society.

Matilda was pleased. Being even more determined than Aunt Eleanor to promote Miss Cummins' restoration, Jessica was being a pattern-card of demure behaviour. She was encouraging her friend to join them at as many social engagements as she could, and Matilda could simply relax and enjoy them.

The snow continued on and off for days, beginning to pile up in high banks, made even higher when servants hurried out from all the houses between snowfalls to clear sufficient room for their employers' carriages.

Charles had heard that the poorer parts of town were almost impassable to wheeled traffic, and reports circulated of people found frozen to death. The workhouses were overwhelmed with people seeking shelter. Even those who could show evidence of their connection to the relevant parish, and who therefore must be supported, were three or more to a bed. Those who couldn't prove their right to relief soon filled all available casual spaces, so that others had to be turned from the gates.

Charles joined several of his friends in asking around the clubs for otherwise empty properties that could provide some shelter for those who otherwise would freeze in an alley. Aldridge was organising the campaign with the Marquess of Glenaire, the Earl of Chadbourn and others, but Charles had no doubt that the Duchess of Haverford was behind it. Certainly, Charles's mother was behind his involvement. She had joined the Society for the Care of Widows and who knew what else was in the ridiculously long name. The Society had a list of ex-soldiers and ex-sailors and their families, and a separate list of widows with children, and would not rest until all were comfortably housed somewhere warm.

Charles dutifully escorted his mother to several meetings of the Society. He'd given up trying to convince himself that seeing the elder Miss Grenford played no part in his willingness to oblige his mother, though his stated excuse was true, too, of course. "The ways are so treacherous, Mother. I will not leave it to a hireling to make sure you are safe."

Today, they'd come once again to Miss Clemens' Book Palace and Tea Rooms. Charles browsed for a book while he waited, then found his way to the tea rooms. Quite a number of men he knew were sitting at the tables, presumably here with the same purpose as his. His friend the Earl of Hythe, brother to Lady Felicity Belvoir, was reading a newspaper while drinking coffee.

He pulled out a chair at the same table. "Hythe," he said, in greeting. "I heard you were out of town."

Hythe looked up and folded the newspaper. "Hamner. I suppose you brought your mother to this interminable charity meeting. I arrived yesterday, and was roped into escort duty immediately." He added, with a shade of embarrassment, "Felicity is in there."

For the past year, Charles and Hythe had not discussed Charles's unsuccessful courtship of Hythe's sister, nor had the subject come up, since Charles had avoided any event Lady Felicity might attend. Charles, cautiously prodding his feelings about greeting the lady, realized that somewhere in the past year any attachment to her had faded into a friendly interest.

If it had ever been anything more, said the inner devils that insisted he felt more for Miss Grenford than was comfortable.

"I haven't seen her for some time," he replied to Hythe. "I trust she and your other sister are well?" He ordered another cup and poured himself a coffee as they chattered about Felicity and Hythe's older sister, Sophia Lady Sutton, who had just been delivered of a daughter. Charles had made an ass of himself when he assumed Lady Sophia's suitor was courting Lady Felicity. He was, on the whole, pleased that the Suttons were in the country for Lady Sutton's confinement.

As if he'd heard the thought, Hythe said, "They'll be in town by the end of the month." He fiddled with his cup before adding, somewhat wistfully, "They are so happy. They married for love. Have you ever thought of such a thing, Hamner? Not that they weren't perfectly matched. He's heir to a duke and Belvoirs can look as high as they like. But love… It seems a risky business."

Charles's shake of the head was more wonderment than nega-tion. "There is almost a fashion. The Suttons are lucky. There was nothing against their marriage except that ancient feud between Haverford and Winshire. To have love on top of it…" A man didn't expect to be in love with his wife — he wanted good breeding, a pristine reputation, sufficient intelligence that he need not fear for the wits of his heir. He owed his wife respect, yes, and a familial affection. But romantic love?

Hythe was nodding. "And then you look at the Chirburys — all those children and still they raise the temperature of the room just by looking at one another across it."

"Hence all the children." Charles's remark got the laugh he was looking for, but it did not lighten Hythe's mood.

"The meeting must be almost over," the other peer said. "Shall we go and wait outside the door?"

They took up station outside the meeting room, nodding to the other men who were also waiting.

"The Thames is the worst I've seen it for ice," one of the others said.

"They can't get barges or boats past London Bridge at all," another commented.

"The weather has to clear, surely?" said a third. "It's just two and half weeks until the Society's big event. I'm looking forward to the auction!"

Hythe made a low-voiced remark under cover of the laughter. "I hope she is somewhere safe out of the cold."

He was talking to himself but Charles felt compelled to comment. "Someone important to you? Can I help?"

Hythe flashed him a smile that reached no further than a quirk of the lips. "The widow of a friend. I arrived back yesterday to a letter telling me she had arrived back in England and planned to stay at his family home, but they have not seen her, and neither have her own family. According to the Horse Guard, she reached England, but they have no further information. Nothing anyone can do except wait for her to write again, I suppose." This woman meant more to Hythe than he was admitting. Charles thought of asking another question and then let it go. It was not his business.

The other men were debating which picnic baskets to buy, some leaning towards the lady with the best cook, and others to the one with whom they wished to spend time. "I'm told the Society has taken measure to ensure the ladies will be well chaperoned," said one gentleman.

His sigh fetched another laugh, interrupted when the meeting room door opened, and the ladies began to stream out, all talking with great excitement. Charles heard mention of the Thames, and a marquee, and the need to transport large carpets. Then his mother reached him, arm in arm with the elder Grenford sister. With his focus on the female who bedevilled his dreams, he hardly noticed Hythe as the man nodded a farewell and went to meet his sister.

"It is decided then," Lady Hamner said, just before she noticed Charles. "There you are, dear. You know my son, do you not, Miss Grenford? Charles, Miss Grenford and I have been charged with making lists of all the things we will need to have ready in case the Thames freezes hard enough to walk on. I have offered room in your warehouse down by Blackfriars Bridge, subject to your approval, so we may be ready at a moment's notice to put up everything we will need. This is very exciting!"

Her enthusiasm was such that Charles had to smile. "You may have room in the warehouse, of course, Mother. But for what, may a mere male ask?"

"An alternative venue, dear," Lady Hamner said. She was looking around with the vague expression that signalled she had just remembered something. "Excuse me, Miss Grenford, would you? I had one more matter I wished to discuss with Her Grace. Charles, you don't mind waiting with Miss Grenford, do you?"

Without pausing for an answer, she headed back into the meeting room. Charles smiled at Miss Grenford. "For what do you need an alternative venue?" he asked.

She returned his smile, her eyes dancing, and his breath caught. She was unbelievably lovely. "For the Venetian Breakfast and Auction, Lord Hamner. If the Thames is frozen on the third of February, we plan to hold it on the ice."

He was silent a moment, picturing it. If anyone could put such an audacious plan into spectacularly successful action, it would be this particular group of ladies. "The ball, too?" he asked. That might be harder to implement. But no, Miss Grenford was shaking her head.

"The ball will be at Haverford House, as planned. If the freeze continues, though, we will erect a large marquee on the Thames and hold the auction there, with small tents around it just large enough for groups to eat whatever they win in their picnic baskets."

She gave a little jump of excitement, and blushed at her lapse of decorum. "I do hope it freezes," she said.

5

Heavy snow falls in the next few days kept the Grenford sisters and their guest indoors. On the first fine day, Matilda, Jessica and Miss Cummins set off for Hyde Park in the company of Lord Trehallow and Lord Hamner. The carriage had some difficulty negotiating the streets, heaped with snow on either side where it had been pushed off the roofs to protect them from collapsing.

They were meeting friends to skate on the iced over Serpentine, and the going got easier the closer they came to the open spaces of the park. In small groups of three or four, they set out on the ice. Deep in conversation, Matilda suddenly realized that Jessica had left her friends. Her deep wine redingote was unmistakable as the wearer steadily skated alone on the ice, almost out of sight around a curve.

On the path, two men were running in and out of the people who thronged the park, enjoying the fine weather after so many days inside. Aldridge's men, presumably, but on foot, had not been able to keep up with the skater.

Matilda excused herself to follow her sister. She had not cleared the cluster of skaters she knew before she realized that another person was keeping pace with her on her left. The frisson of awareness warned her of his identity before a glance to her side confirmed it.

"You are following your sister?" Lord Hamner asked.

She was about to snap that it was none of his concern, but Aldridge's insinuation gave her pause. Instead, her voice was mild when she answered. "I am. She is outpacing her footmen, and she may not realize." Let Hamner understand that the Grenford sisters had protectors close at hand.

She expected the arrogant man to rebuke her, but his response was polite, and almost tentative. "May I escort you, Miss Grenford? I promise not to interfere, unless she is in danger."

"Very well," she found herself saying. The thought of possible danger had her increasing her speed, but Lord Hamner kept pace beside her. "Thank you," she added.

When the next stretch of the Serpentine came into view, Matilda was nowhere in sight. No. Wait — there, on the bank, she was walking with a gentleman. As she and Lord Hamner drew closer, he hissed, "Driscoll!"

"You know the gentleman?" she asked.

"He is no gentlemen," Lord Hamner said, as he skidded to a halt at the bank and stopped to untie his skates. "We must hurry."

Matilda was delayed by trying to keep sight of her sister while undoing her skates, and was several yards behind Lord Hamner as he hurried across the snowy path in pursuit of the couple.

He had not reached them when Jessica drew away from Mr. Driscoll, saying words that did not reach Matilda, though the sharp tone did. Mr. Driscoll did not accept his dismissal. He grabbed Jessica's arm before she could escape, and tugged her towards him, so that she lost her balance on the snow and fell towards him, clutching at him to stay upright.

Before the man could take advantage of Jessica's forced embrace, Lord Hamner was upon them. Mr. Driscoll found himself dragged backwards. Jessica, released so suddenly she almost fell again, caught her balance, saw Matilda, and threw herself into Matilda's arms.

Lord Hamner interrupted his low-voiced argument with Mr.

Driscoll to say to Matilda, "Get her away, Miss Grenford. You should not be part of the scene."

Matilda looked around to see that the altercation had drawn the attention of others in the park. Just then, the two Haverford footmen she had seen earlier arrived, breathing heavily from their exertion. Two more were approaching. She had not realized that Aldridge had watchers on her, too.

"Come, Jess," she said. "Let us return to our friends."

Followed by the four footmen, they collected their skates from the water's edge, and headed along the path towards their starting point. Matilda turned back at the corner, and was just in time to see Lord Hamner fetch Mr. Driscoll a mighty punch.

"Leave Miss Grenford alone, or I'll rearrange your face for you, and then leave you to Lord Aldridge's mercies," Charles warned Driscoll.

"What business is it of yours," Driscoll snarled. "The bitch was just playing coy, but she wanted me. Why else would she come to meet me?"

Charles glared. "Good question. How did you inveigle her? She was not welcoming your attentions, that is certain." He had seen blind panic on Miss Jessica's face at the moment she realised Driscoll was not taking 'no' for an answer.

"She wanted it," Driscoll insisted, but his eyes shifted away from Charles's. "She was pretending to protest. Women do that."

"Leave her alone," Charles repeated.

"Come on!" Driscoll pasted on a smile. "All this fuss over a woman like her?" The smile slipped to a leer. "This is what they're born to, Charles, and everyone knows it. Even the duchess will have to face facts in time. Aldridge is a man of the world. He indulges his mother, but he certainly doesn't expect men to leave two such honey-pots alone."

"You are mistaken, Driscoll. He expects it, and so do I." Charles grabbed the stupid man by the capes that adorned the shoulders of his heavy overcoat and pulled him closer, so he could hiss his final warning straight into the man's face. "Leave. The. Grenford. Ladies. Alone."

Driscoll struggled ineffectually, his face reddening in his anger. Still, he continued to sneer. "Want both of them, do you? What's it like, tupping the Ice Princess? Does she freeze your d—"

Charles dropped the man's coat and stopped his foul mouth with a punch that sent him reeling backwards. Driscoll landed splayed in a snow bank, flecks of blood spattering the white beside his head. He opened his eyes and glared at Charles, but made no effort to more.

Itching to haul the villain to his feet and repeat the blow, Charles forced himself to remember the Grenford sisters. He should make sure they were unharmed. He should escort them home. "Remember what I said," he ordered, and turned away, allowing himself a wince and a certain satisfaction. The bruising his gloved hand had suffered was a rather nice indication of the damage to Driscoll's face.

When he looked back before rounding the corner of the path, Driscoll was gone.

Miss Grenford and Miss Jessica had not re-joined their group. Instead, they had found a bench and were talking earnestly while the footmen hovered. They didn't prevent Charles from approaching. Instead, his rescue of Miss Jessica won him nods of greeting from the watchful guardians.

"I thought the note was from someone who could help Lady— my friend," Miss Jessica was saying. Charles glanced at the piece of paper she handed to her sister.

'I have what you were seeking in Berkley Street. Skate north. You will find me around the corner wearing a red cockade in my hat. Red for love.'

"I don't understand it," Miss Jessica said to Miss Grenford. "I asked him what information he had about... What information he had, and he would not say. He wanted me to go with him somewhere warm, where we could..." She shook her head as if to dispel Driscoll's words, and Charles wished he had punched him harder.

"He kept saying whatever I got at Berkley Street, he could give me better, but I did not get anything there. I take them food and clothing, and money when I have some. I do not expect anything from them." Miss Jessica took the note back from Miss Grenford's hand and stared at it in confusion.

"Driscoll knows nothing of your real purpose, Miss Jessica," Charles told her. "Nor do I, come to that, but I do not share his assumptions." Or, at least, not any more. Whatever took her to a scruffy middle-class street in Clerkenwell, it was not a tryst with a lover.

"His assumptions?" Miss Jessica looked from Charles to Miss Grenford, her brows drawn together in confusion. As his meaning dawned on her, her eyes widened and she flushed. "How dare he! I have never even met the man! Why would he think...? O-o-o-h!" She stamped her foot in her anger.

"He saw you coming out of the house you have been visiting in Berkley Street," Charles explained.

Miss Grenford's eyes narrowed. "How do you know this, Lord Hamner? Is he a friend of yours?"

Charles threw up a hand in rejection of the accusation. "Indeed not! He is a careless rakehell whose dissolute lifestyle has so far not crossed the line enough to have him banned from Polite Society. Enough, though, that no hostess would dare Her Grace's anger to introduce him to you. No, I overheard him boasting at Lady Parkinson's soiree. He said he had tried to catch her, but she escaped him in the fog."

Miss Jessica paled as her eyes widened. "That was him? Mercy! I very nearly stopped to ask him to help me find the way home!"

Miss Grenford spoke at the same time, lifting both brows and nodding her head. "That is what you were trying to tell me when we were dancing! Why on earth did you not say so?"

The last thing Charles wanted was to tell her the truth, that his wits went begging as soon as he touched her. Instead, he chose to answer her sister. "Just as well you did not, Miss Jessica. He is not to be trusted."

"So I just found. Oh no!" Miss Jessica turned to Miss Grenford, gripping her arm with both hands. "Tilda, he is Amhurst's brother-in-law! What if he goes to Berkley Street?" She spun on her heel,

saying over her shoulder, "I have to go there now. I have to warn L
—my friend."

Miss Grenford took three swift steps and stopped her with a
hand on her shoulder. "Jessie, you cannot go to Clerkenwell."

"You do not understand." Miss Jessica put her hand over Miss
Grenford's, though she did not go as far as to try to pry up the
fingers. "Even if he does not attack her as he did me… You have no
idea what is at stake."

"Indeed, I do not, for you refused to tell me anything." She cast
a quick glance sideways at Charles, and said, "Tell us how we can
help. You know you can trust me, and Lord Hamner has shown
himself to be a true friend."

Charles warmed as the words struck home and felt a burning
desire to prove himself worthy of the accolade. He nodded to Miss
Jessica, doing his best to look both reliable and unthreatening. "Why
not write your friend a letter, Miss Jessica, and I will carry it to her?
The streets in Clerkenwell will be even harder to negotiate than
here, outside of town, so going by carriage will not be an option."

Matilda added her persuasion. "You know Aldridge will not
permit you to go back to Clerkenwell."

Miss Jessica paused in thought, and Charles and Miss Grenford
waited. At last, the younger sister nodded as she came to some kind
of decision. "It will be sunset in less than an hour," she noted. "Lord
Hamner, if you are really willing to help, will you come to Haverford House early tomorrow and escort my friend Miss Cummins to
deliver that letter? She has to go in that direction, because she is
almoner at The Benevolent Pauper's Hospital of the Apostles, and
you will be there to keep her safe."

Charles not only escorted Miss Cummins to Clerkenwell the
following morning, he waited outside in the sleigh his coachman
had unearthed from the back of the carriage house so he could take
her on to the hospital.

Despite the blankets and furs he'd ordered piled up in the sleigh,
it was a cold wait. Colder still for the coachman up on his perch in

front, though he was swaddled in an enormous coat, with a hat pulled down over his ears and the lower part of his face hidden in layers of scarf. Even the footman Charles had brought for extra security was possibly warmer than Charles, who had his face mostly exposed as he watched the narrow terrace house into which Miss Cummins had disappeared.

It seemed much longer than the actual twenty minutes that elapsed before she emerged, clambering over a bank of snow to where they waited in the narrow cleared path in the centre of the street. Charles managed to struggle out of his covers and was waiting beside the sleigh to hand her in by the time she reached him.

"Success?" he asked. He had agreed to return after taking Miss Cummins to the hospital, and provide transport back to Haverford House for Miss Jessica's friend and a child, if the lady agreed. But Miss Cummins shook her head. "She has written a letter to Jess, my lord. She says you are not to come back."

Charles instructed the coachman to return to Haverford House by way of the hospital. The sleigh made the trip possible, but not comfortable, and the snow was starting again, just lazy swirls of insubstantial crystals that seemed far too ephemeral to be so close to shutting down the city, not to mention the countryside.

Back at Haverford House, he gave Miss Jessica her letter. She opened it eagerly and read it, but from the look of her face, the news was not what she hoped for. Matilda laid a consoling hand on her arm.

"She is leaving Berkley Street. She says she has another place in mind, out of London. She asks me to keep my silence for two more days." Miss Jessica took a deep breath and heaved a sigh as she threw up her hands, the letter in one hand rustling as it flapped.

"She cannot have thought… The snow, the roads. And what if I find someone who knows…? Lord Hamner, would you be kind enough to take me back there? Now? Tilda, will you tell the duchess I am with Lord Hamner and safe?"

Nothing Miss Grenford said soothed Miss Jessica's agitation, and before long, Charles had retrieved his poor coachman and several stout footmen from the Haverford kitchens and was once again traversing the near silent streets. Aldridge would have his head on a platter for helping his sister to disobey a direct prohibition.

In any case, it was to no avail. When they finally arrived at Berkley Street, the landlady reported that Miss Jessica's friend had packed up all her things and left.

6

"The snow makes everything much harder, Miss Grenford," complained the carrier, as he lugged another heavy packing case of bunting — swathe after swathe of fabric in the colours of the Union Flag. Some of the crates held actual flags to be hung, along with the bunting, in the great public rooms of Haverford House, including the ballroom. Not just the British flag, but the more ancient flags that made it up: those of Scotland, England, and Wales.

"It does," Matilda agreed. "Thank you again for agreeing to deliver everything early, so we can be sure of its arrival."

The carrier, blushing at praise from one of the gentry, touched his cap in deference, and went back to shouting at his labourers with renewed vigour.

Matilda hesitated. Someone needed to supervise the delivery, but she had many other things to do. With just over a week until the event, the uncertainty about whether the Venetian Breakfast and auction would be here or on the frozen Thames, and the disruptions caused by the on-again off-again snow, all of the ladies of the committee were filling every possible moment with preparations.

"Lady Hamner is coming early for today's Society for Brat's

meeting," Jessica reminded her, "so that you and she can talk about the things you have ready for the Frost Fair."

"Yes!" Matilda agreed. "I need to bring my lists down and make sure the Unicorn Parlour is ready."

"Go, then, Jessica said. "I can manage here."

Matilda stopped with one foot on the stairs. "I have not forgotten you promised me your explanation for the lady in Clerkenwell today."

"After the Society meeting," Jessica promised. "If Aldridge is here, I can tell him at the same time."

"And Lord Hamner," Matilda suggested. "He will be escorting his mother to the meeting." He had been assiduous in his attendance on his mother since she and Matilda began working together. Matilda thought nothing of it until Lady Hamner commented. Apparently, he had always before been content to send her on her errands and calls around town with a groom and a footman as escort.

"I can guess," Lady Hamner had laughed, "the reason for his sudden devotion." Did she mean that Lord Hamner came to see Matilda? If so, she certainly did not seem to disapprove.

Matilda shook off her preoccupation with the earl and made a speedy trip back up to her chambers for the notes she had made ready for her talk with Lady Hamner and the meeting to follow.

With slightly more than a week to go, it seemed more and more likely they would need the marquees, tents, carpets, and other equipment that they had been collecting in Hamner's warehouse. Vast quantities of ice clogged all the waterways of London, and the weather-wise predicted that the cold would continue.

Heavy drapes had been drawn in the Unicorn Parlour—so called for the unicorns carved into the fire surround, moulded on the ceiling plaster, and pictured in tapestries around the room. A water urn and tea pot stood ready on a side table, and Matilda measured tea from the waiting canister and made the tea so that it would have time to steep before Lady Hamner arrived.

The curtains meant the fire in the hearth had a better chance of keeping the room warm, but the corners were still chilly. Matilda manoeuvred a pair of chairs closer to the hearth. She was busy positioning the second chair when someone spoke from behind her.

"Whom do we have here?" It was the Duke of Haverford. Matilda straightened, turned around, and curtsied. The duke squinted at her. One of his eyes was almost closed by a loathsome growth, under which an open ulcer seeped—outward signs of the disease that was killing him by inches. "Angel?"

"No, Your Grace. It is Matilda."

The duke took no notice, lumbering towards her with his arms out. "Angel! Come here and give me a kiss."

Matilda did her best to evade him, arguing all the time that she was not Angel, but Matilda. "Matilda," she repeated. Desperate, she said the words he refused to allow spoken. "I am your daughter, Your Grace."

His Grace roared, a wordless prolonged bellow of rage, as he grabbed her by both arms and shook her. He pushed her backwards as she struggled, shouting for help, until he had her crowded against the wall, his weight pinning her in place so that, when he let go of her hands, she still could not free herself.

With one hand on her throat, he cut off her breath, and with it her screams. The other hand must be scrabbling at her gown. She felt the chill air first on her calves and then on her knee as he lifted it higher and higher. She flailed with her arms, striking impotently at his head and shoulders as her eyesight blurred and darkness began to close in.

All the while, he muttered obscenities about what he planned, and the frequent endearments to Angel only added to the horror.

Then, of a sudden, she was free, and gasping for breath. As her eyes refocused, and her air-starved brain began to make sense of the scene before her, she saw His Grace send his duchess reeling across the room to fall in a heap against the wall. Behind him, a footman stood indecisive, hesitating to wrestle with his master but reluctant to leave his mistress to the man's non-existent mercies.

"Get Lord Aldridge," Matilda hissed, trying to keep her voice low enough to avoid attracting the duke's attention, but he turned his head towards her, and growled, the sound coming from low in his chest. He began to stalk towards her. She slid along the wall, trying to get further away, though she had little hope she could evade him and reach the door.

Behind him, Aunt Eleanor stirred. Thank God. Matilda had feared the duke had killed her.

"What the devil?" The expostulation came from the doorway. "What's going on here?"

The duke swung his head to glare at Lord Hamner, who was crossing the room in long strides. "Get out!" he commanded. "This is none of your business. The girl is mine."

"He thinks I'm his mistress," Matilda explained. "He struck the duchess."

Lord Hamner's eyes fell to her neck and his eyes blazed. "You have hurt them both, you monster," he told the duke, his voice low and furious.

"Get out, puppy. You have no right to interfere between a man and his pleasure," the duke snarled, and he struck out at Lord Hamner. Matilda winced, but Hamner somehow swayed just far enough that the blow did not land. Instead, His Grace's arm shot past Hamner, who grabbed it and pulled, so that the duke stumbled after his own blow, crashing over a low sofa and falling to the floor beyond.

"Quick. Go to Mother," Hamner told Matilda. Lady Hamner was crouching over Aunt Eleanor, and Matilda hurried around the edges of the room to join them as Hamner vaulted over the sofa to thump the duke on the back of his head as he began to get up.

Matilda tried to keep one eye on their fight while assisting Lady Hamner with the duchess, who was trying to sit up, declaring that she was perfectly fine while half swooning in their supporting arms.

Then, suddenly, it was over.

Aldridge entered the room, took in the scene with a single glance, and ordered the three hefty men who crowded after him into action. Matilda didn't recognize them. Their sober clothing suggested they were upper servants, but their burly physiques spoke of some more vigorous profession. In moments, the duke was struggling under a pile of all three.

"Laudanum," Aldridge instructed. Matilda couldn't see details through the melee, but he must have been obeyed, because the duke suddenly went limp. Aldridge ignored the men who were now untangling themselves and standing, and reached out a hand to help Lord Hamner to his feet. "My thanks." Several swift strides brought him to his mother's side. He crouched, reaching out a hand to gently skim the bruise that was rapidly purpling the side of her face.

"I beg your pardon, Mama. He should never have been able to evade his watchers." He narrowed his eyes at the men, who were now lifting the duke between them and carrying him towards the door. "I shall find out what happened and it shan't happen again." One of the men met his gaze. "My lord—"

"Later, Stebbings," Aldridge growled, and the men left, shutting the door behind them.

The duchess patted his shoulder, soothing him as she would a frightened child. "I am a little bruised, my son, and nothing worse." She met Matilda's eyes, a question in them.

"I am well, Aunt Eleanor." Her voice was a little husky. She cleared her throat, hiding a wince at the pain from her bruising. "You intervened before any harm was done."

The duchess made to get up, and with Aldridge on one side of her and Lord Hamner on the other, she managed to rise. They supported her to the nearest sofa, and Matilda and Lady Hamner followed. The duchess was insisting she was perfectly well.

"I will just rest for a few minutes, and I will be perfectly ready for the meeting of the Society."

Matilda murmured to Aldridge, "She was knocked out for a moment, Aldridge."

"Mama, I want a doctor to examine you," Aldridge told the duchess. "That was quite a bang on your head."

"I want no fuss," Aunt Eleanor insisted. She looked thoughtfully at Lord Hamner, and then at Lady Hamner, who had made her a cup of tea and was bringing it to her.

"I had a fall," she declared. "Most clumsy of me."

"Yes, Eleanor," Lady Hamner agreed. "Hamner and I will say nothing to the contrary, you can be sure. I assume your servants will keep silent?"

Aunt Eleanor put out a hand to draw the other lady down beside her. "Aldridge's men will not speak of this, Clara, and I know

I can trust you and your son. Lord Hamner, we owe you a debt for your intervention."

The edge to Aldridge's voice, and the restless flexing of one hand, were the only indications of his distress. "The men will explain how His Grace came to be here, alone, and in a condition to attack my mother and my sister. But yes, they will be silent, though it won't be necessary for much longer. I have also spoken to the footman you sent for me, Matilda. He will not betray us."

Hamner was as tense as Aldridge. "And how will you make sure that your father is not again enabled to attack Miss— to attack the ladies? The man was trying to—"

Aldridge interrupted; his tone arctic. "Thank you, Hamner. I am aware, but we do not need to further distress the ladies."

"Do not be concerned, Hamner," Aunt Eleanor said. "As soon as the hearing is over, His Grace will be confined at Haverford Castle."

"Mama!" Aldridge protested.

"Calm yourself, my dear." The duchess was back to her usual dignified self. "Clara is my friend, and Hamner is… a fine gentleman, and has been friend to us all, especially today. After what they have witnessed, and what poor Matilda has been through, they deserve to know that we are taking measures to have His Grace declared incompetent. We do not want the matter discussed until the result is decided, Clara."

Aldridge sighed. "I had the duke brought from Haverford Castle to be present at the hearing. The deterioration in his mind is obvious to anyone who speaks with him, so it can only help. Today was the last day of presenting evidence, and he will return to the castle as soon as the roads are passable. Nor do I expect them to linger over the decision."

"If it helps," Hamner offered, "I would be willing to testify about what I observed."

The duchess sipped her tea, as if discussions of competence hearings were perfectly normally drawing room conversations. Aldridge answered Hamner, but his voice seemed to come from a long way away. Matilda's heart raced as if she were still under attack, her skin felt clammy and there seemed too little air in the room. She did not realize she was swaying until Hamner was there, his solid presence anchoring her to the room. He helped her to a chair.

"You are safe," he assured her. "Just sit here and take a deep breath. Here. My mother has made you a cup of tea: a little bit of cream and one teaspoon of sugar, just how you like it."

Hamner knew how she took her tea. Wasn't that nice?

"He thought I was my mother," she told him. Tears filled her eyes. "I have tried so hard to be a lady, but people only ever see my mother."

"Not I," Hamner assured her, crouching at her side and taking her free hand. "I see a lady to admire; one who reminds me very much of the fine lady who raised her. I see a lady with excellent manners, high moral standards, and a kind, generous heart. You have the beauty of the woman who birthed you, Miss Matilda Grenford, but you are far more than the offspring of that man and his mistress. In every way that counts, you are the daughter of Her Grace, the Duchess of Haverford."

"Hear, hear," said Lady Hamner and Aunt Eleanor, in chorus. Their support frayed the last of Matilda's self-control, and she found herself crying, in great wrenching gulps. On the granite earl's shoulder, too. Who would have thought it?

7

"Will you give your testimony now, while it is fresh in your mind?" Aldridge asked, and when Charles agreed, Aldridge asked him to wait a moment while he made arrangements.

First, the marquis insisted on his mother and sister retiring to their chambers while he sent for a doctor. Matilda, after she'd spent her tears, went without complaint, though she assured Charles's mother she would call on her tomorrow for the conversation they had missed today.

The duchess made more difficulty, but Lady Hamner countered every one of her arguments for carrying on, pointing out that Her Grace needed to consider the lacerated feelings of her son, that the other ladies of the Society were well equipped to meet without her, that Lady Hamner herself would report after the meeting so that the duchess knew what had taken place, and that the duchess was not showing much confidence in the abilities of those she herself had appointed.

Defeated, she agreed to see the doctor and to follow his advice.

Charles waited, helping his mother to restore the room to rights before the ladies arrived for the meeting. A footman came to conduct him to Aldridge's study just in time for him to avoid the first arrivals. He felt far from ready to speak social nothings.

In the study he found the marquis had already produced a lawyer to take Charles's testimony. Aldridge was not there, but he returned as the lawyer packed up the signed and witnessed statement.

Aldridge showed the lawyer to the door, then crossed to a well-stocked shelf of decanters.

"You'll be ready for a brandy, Charles. The doctor suggests Mama and Matilda both rest, and he will return to see how they are tomorrow. Bruising, he assures us, and some shock, of course." His lip twisted in a quick smile. "Mama told him that she has not survived to this age by allowing small inconveniences to overset her."

"I am sorry," Charles said. "That business the year before last when His Grace tried to kill Winshire's sons… It was beginning then?"

Aldridge shook his head. "He has been having… spells of madness on and off for several years. Rarely, and then more often. He used to recover after a few hours, then days, then weeks. This time… It has been three months, and the duchy cannot continue with him at its helm. I have his proxy to do most things, but he can countermand my orders at any time, and I cannot trust that my control will continue to prevail."

Aldridge sounded almost apologetic. "You are doing the right thing," Charles assured him. "Today… I was never more shocked. He was… I always looked up to him, Aldridge. He was generous with his time, charming, and so willing to share his knowledge with a boy who succeeded to a title before he was ready."

Aldridge saluted Charles with his glass. "You saw a different side to him than his wife and children. In public, he was everything you say. *En famille*, he has always been erratic and tyrannical. I used to envy you and Hythe, and others of his disciples. But in the end, perhaps I had the better part, since I never expected enough of him to be disappointed."

Charles had nothing to say to that harsh assessment.

Aldridge offered him a wry smile. "I have shocked you. I solicit your pardon, Charles. I am a little overset myself."

"I do not wonder at it. That scene…" Charles could not

complete the sentence, shaking his head as he remembered the indescribable rage that surged through him when he opened the door and saw the duke attacking Matilda.

"Would have been worse had you not happened along when you did. Another minute or two— I shudder to think I might have been too late. I am deeply in your debt, Charles. It must have been hard for you, to fight the man you so admire."

Not hard at all. He did not recall giving the matter a single thought. As soon as his eyes registered Matilda's plight, his only goal was to see her safe, and no past history with the duke would have stayed his hand even to murder, had that been needed.

"I hope I would always come to the rescue of ladies in danger," he said. It was not a lie, but it was at least a prevarication. Between his arrival in that doorway and the moment he took Matilda's hand after making her a cup of tea, his awareness had shifted; his sense of himself and his goals changing, as if he had leapt a hedge and landed in a whole new landscape, quite different from the first.

Matilda—he could no longer keep her at a distance, even in his own mind, by thinking of her as Miss Grenford—was his lady. His to protect and to serve. Whether he could ever be her lord remained to be seen. Most of the time, as far as he could see, she didn't even like him.

She had cried on his shoulder, it was true, but his was the nearest one available.

She had invited him into her quest to help her sister, but again, he was at hand and ready to help.

A knock on the door heralded the arrival of a footman with a message. Miss Grenford and Miss Jessica asked Lord Aldridge and Lord Hamner to step up to the sisters' sitting room, as Miss Jessica had a story she had promised to tell today.

Aldridge raised one elegant eyebrow. "My sisters' *private* sitting room? Is there something you need to tell me, Hamner?"

Charles was already on his feet. "It is two days later," he explained, then realized how obscure the remark was. "Miss Jessica's friend in Clerkenwell asked her to keep her secret for two days. May I...? I don't suppose Matil— Miss Grenford wishes to come downstairs given..." he waved one hand in a helpless effort to convey bruising and shock.

Aldridge's sigh was near theatrical. "I suppose Sir Galahad should hear the end of the tale. This way, Hamner."

In the pretty sitting room, feminine without being fussy, Matilda had changed her gown for one with a high neck, and had further folded a light gauze scarf about her throat so that the bruises no longer showed. She was pale but composed, and met Charles's anxious gaze with a smile. "Thank you for coming."

Miss Jessica sat beside her sister, holding her hand. Just as well, or Charles might have appropriated the place, and if he had been that close to Matilda he could not have resisted touching her. He should probably keep his distance until he had the savage feelings aroused by seeing her in danger under some sort of control.

Charles took the seat to which he was directed, but Aldridge ignored the wave of Matilda's hand and sat on the arm of her sofa. Dropping his usual bored sardonic air, the marquis bent over his sister. "How are you, Matilda? Are you up to this?"

"Do not fuss over me, too, Aldridge. I will keep busy, and I will be perfectly well. I am more worried about Aunt Eleanor. The doctor said she is not badly hurt and will quickly recover, but what did he tell you?"

Aldridge patted the hand that was not resting in Jessica's. "The same. Do not be concerned, dear one. The doctor is not, and neither is Mama."

Matilda turned her eyes to Charles. "I need to thank you, my lord. I shudder to think what might have happened had you delayed coming to my aid."

Charles reassured her he was always at her service. Even if she took it as a mere form of words, he hoped that later he could convince her of his sincerity. Not today. Not while she was still recovering from the horror of the attack.

"I should leave you to your recovery, Miss Grenford," he offered, but she shook her head.

"Jessica promised that she would explain about the friend in Clerkenwell today, and I am determined to hear the story. I thought you would wish it, too. Aldridge also needs to know—if he has not already been informed by those he sets to watch us." She arched one eyebrow at the marquis, a smile playing around her lips, the gesture enhancing the slight familial resemblance between half-brother and sister.

"Watchers?" Jessica's eyes widened. "Aldridge!"

"For our safety," Matilda scolded, "and do not deny it has been necessary, Jessie."

Jessica blushed. "I do not know where to start."

"The beginning is usually an excellent place." Even the tone was that of Matilda's brother, though in a more feminine register.

Jessica raised her own eyebrow, but obediently began, "In October, I met a friend while visiting repatriated widows at St Swithins. Do you remember Anne Pembroke, Matilda? Who disappeared during our first season?"

Matilda nodded. Aldridge said, "The Pembroke girl? Wasn't she brought out by an aunt then sent home in disgrace when she was caught kissing Amhurst's son in a garden?"

Charles nodded. He remembered the scandal. Amhurst had proclaimed that his son was already betrothed and, just like that, the girl was ruined.

"By my recollection," Aldridge said. "The betrothal came to nothing; if it existed in truth. I never heard the name of the supposed betrothed mentioned."

"Then Amhurst's son joined a Hussar regiment," Charles mused. "Unusual in the heir to an heir of an earl. I don't know what happened to the girl."

"She was sent to an aunt in Scotland," Jessica explained. "It is her I have been helping. Her and her son."

"Poor girl," he commented.

"You said she was with the war widows." Aldridge was leaning forward, his gaze intent. "Did she marry a soldier, Jess?"

Matilda frowned. "Two years ago, she had no eyes for anyone but Mr. Marbeck, but I suppose if she was with child..."

"She married Marbeck, Tilda. She ran away. A friend of Marbeck's gave her money for her passage to Spain, and Marbeck had servants and transport waiting for her when she arrived. He wed her as soon as she reached his brigade, and she followed the drum until he died of a fever somewhere in the mountains between Spain and France…" she paused, and then sprung the last of the story on them, her voice dropping to a thrilled hum. "just a day before the letter came telling him his father and grandfather had died, and he was now earl."

Charles met Aldridge's eyes. Aldridge had realized the same thing as him and put it into words. "Amhurst's brother has been named Earl, but if his nephew married and had a son…"

Charles completed the thought. "Amhurst's brother was estranged from his father and brother, and living in obscurity. He has married on the strength of his new wealth and his title. I doubt he will like being supplanted by his great nephew."

"You may be sure of his displeasure," Jessica said. "Lady Amhurst, as she is now, wrote to him as well as to her own parents, but with no reply. After I spoke to the new earl's wife, though, they came and took her and the boy home to their townhouse, and I thought all would be well."

It wasn't. In pieces, interrupted by questions, Jessica told of Lady Amhurst approaching her in the street outside the hospital, begging for help. The uncle-in-law had refused to believe in her marriage, and had had her escorted from the house, but not before taking her son. "He may be a bastard, but he is family," the man had told her.

The distraught mother, convinced that the false earl meant the boy no good, had gone to her parents for help, but they, too, had turned her away, telling her that she had brought her troubles on herself and that the child was better off with the earl, his great uncle.

So, Jessica and Lady Amhurst had stolen the child back. Matilda's hair rose on the back of her neck as she listened to Jessica's audacious plan; arriving at the townhouse dressed as servants when the false Amhursts were entertaining, and sneaking up to the top floor, where they found little Sammie, hungry and cold, crying alone in a dark nursery. Lady Amhurst had gone into hiding, and Jessica had been searching for anyone among the soldiers or camp followers back from the wars for someone who had witnessed the wedding.

"The marriage should be noted in the regimental records,"

Aldridge told her. "Young Marbeck would have needed permission from his regimental commander, both to wed and to keep his wife with him. I'll see what I can find out, Jess."

Jessica clung to Matilda's hand, her voice small. "I should have told you before. I have made a mess of things, trying to do it all myself."

"You were sworn to secrecy, you said," Matilda reminded her.

"She was so frightened, you see. She was still weak from being ill, and she was sure that other people in Society would reject her as her in-laws and then her family did. Amhurst told her that she could not prevent him from taking the child, as he was the head of the family."

"He cannot have it both ways," Aldridge said. "If the child was born outside of marriage, then his mother has sole authority over him. If inside of marriage, then he is the Earl of Amhurst, and his mother the Countess of Amhurst, and due all the respect of that position. Did Lady Amhurst's husband name a guardian for the boy? Things would be simpler if he did so, as long as he didn't choose his uncle."

"Three, but the only one in England hasn't replied to her letter. The other two are both still with the army somewhere in the south of France," Jessica said. "They're no use to her there."

On the contrary. Not only did that mean the uncle had no authority over the boy or his mother, but also no decisions could be imposed on the widowed Countess without first talking to one of the soldiers, and if it took a month or two, that was all to the good.

"It makes a considerable difference, Jess," Aldridge answered. "The uncle has no authority over the boy or his mother."

"True," Charles agreed. "Furthermore, no decisions about the boy's welfare can be imposed on the widow without first talking to at least two of the guardians."

Aldridge nodded. "Yes, and if it takes a month or two to get a message into the war zone and back out again, that's all to the good."

"See? I should have told you," Jessica repeated. "I thought I could do something good; something important by myself. Make a real difference. Instead, Lady Amhurst had disappeared, and who knows how she will manage?"

"If I remember Anne Pembroke, she will have a plan," Matilda soothed.

Charles agreed. "By your account, Miss Jessica, she escaped her family and ran away to Spain, followed the drum for two years, brought herself and her son back from Spain even though she was bereaved and ill, and then stole her son from his great-uncle's house. I would say she has considerable resilience."

Something Miss Jessica had said started a hare in his thoughts. Hythe had mentioned a widow arriving from somewhere overseas, and a letter that awaited him in London. Better to say nothing now in case one lost widow was not the same person as the other. He'd call on Hythe and check it out.

Aldridge had gone on talking. "Jess, you'll need to wait for her to get in touch. Meanwhile, we can make a start on resolving the matter. We can find out who the brigade commander is, and where his is, and make sure of the guardianship matter, at least. Hamner, we should leave the ladies to prepare for their evening entertainments."

Charles gave Matilda a concerned look. "Are you planning to go out? Even after… Are you sure you are well enough?"

"I would not miss it for the world," Matilda assured him. "Merchant of Venice is one of my favourite plays. And Jess and Percy are looking forward to it, too."

Charles had to leave it at that, since Aldridge made no demur and Charles did not have the authority to cosset Matilda as he would wish. The thought stole unbidden into his mind: not yet.

"Aldridge," he asked, "may I have a word before I go?"

8

Aldridge took advantage of the misty thaw the next day to move the duke to Haverford Castle on the north coast of Kent near Margate. He had tentative guardianship, pending a final decision by a committee of the House of Lords and ratification by the Prince Regent. No one doubted the outcome. The attack on Matilda, the reports of several doctors, and Haverford's own raving incomprehension when he appeared before the hearing all favoured the decision to place one of the kingdom's foremost duchies in safer hands.

"I'll be gone several days," Aldridge told Matilda. "I understand the roads are dreadful, so I do not expect to make good time. I hope Mama will keep to her rooms today, but I don't suppose you or I can insist that she does so."

Her Grace was resting, her dresser told Matilda. She wanted no fuss, and would be well directly. Matilda could not help a smile at the message, delivered in a flawless imitation of Aunt Eleanor's tone. "Please make sure I am told if she wishes us to visit, or if she has any tasks we may do for her," she said. "Oh, and do send me a message if she decides to get up."

The dresser, a long-standing and trusted servant, complained that even Miss Tilda would not be able to stop Her Grace if she took it into her head to overdo things, "but I will let you know, Miss Tilda, you can be sure."

"We need to make the most of the fine weather," Jessica declared, "Though I hope it doesn't last overlong. Every day of warmer temperatures makes the Frost Fair less likely."

She and Miss Cummins hurried off about errands to do with the charity event, leaving Matilda to take a pen and notebook down into the reception rooms to note what furniture needed to be moved into another part of the house, or down for use at the auction, the breakfast, or the ball.

As they had it planned, the ballroom could be set up the day before, all except for fresh flowers, which would need to be delivered and arranged on the morning of the Third of February.

The grand dining room would also be prepared on the Second to entertain those guests invited to join the duchess for dinner before the ball.

Indeed, work on both rooms had already begun, as well as the withdrawing rooms for ladies and gentlemen, set up in parlours at the extreme ends of the central wing.

The other rooms—a long gallery, three major salons and a series of smaller parlours—would be needed for the afternoon's auction and Breakfast, if the ice did not allow the alternative venue. After each was cleared of guests, servants would need to rapidly make the necessary changes—to supper room, card rooms, a couple of rooms for quiet conversation.

Matilda had apprenticed to her guardian at enough major events to be able to write lists of the possible problems with ideas on how to solve them, and by early afternoon, she was satisfied that, whatever the weather did, they could cope.

She visited the duchess again, and this time was invited inside. Her Grace was dressed, but lying propped up on pillows on a sofa in her sitting room, her eye swollen nearly shut by a large purple bruise. Reassured that Matilda was fully recovered, she claimed that she, too, was on the mend.

"I shall be perfectly well by the auction and ball, my dear," she insisted, "but I know you will all fret if I get up too quickly. Indeed, I am still a little shaken, so I shall rest, and you shall be my deputy and run my messages."

"Of course, Aunt Eleanor," Matilda agreed, and explained what she had been doing. By the time she had displayed her list, the duchess had paled and was drooping on her pillows.

"Tell me what is most urgent for me to know," Matilda said, "then I shall go away and let you rest."

"Nothing, Matilda. You are doing an excellent job. Give me a kiss, my dear, and off you go."

Matilda returned downstairs to check a couple of details she'd thought of during her conversation with the duchess. As she came through the door from the family stairs into the grand entrance hall, the butler opened the door to Lord Hamner. She watched him stamp the snow from his boots and step inside, making a joking remark about the cold to the footman who came to collect his coat, muffler, hat, and gloves.

He had been wonderful yesterday. Indeed, ever since they met in the fog just after Christmas, the granite surface seemed to have evaporated: first in irritation, to be sure, but later that heat had turned to a more comforting warmth.

She shook her head at her own foolish heart. His change of attitude probably meant he had stopped blaming her for the kiss he had stolen at the house party at Hollystone Hall a year ago. No. She could not honestly call it stolen. She had both given and received, and she greatly feared she would do it again.

Except that his subsequent actions showed that he would not consider her as a bride, and she would never dishonour the duchess's care for her by allowing a kiss from anyone but a suitor for her hand in marriage. At least, not again.

He noticed her and approached, smiling warmly. "Miss Grenford. I trust you are well? I called to enquire after you and the duchess. I also have some news for Miss Jessica."

"I am well, my lord. The duchess is recovering from her fall, and hopes to be up and about in the next day or two. Jessie has not yet returned from errands, but I was about to take tea. Would you care to join me?"

"I'd like that, very much." He followed her to the Rose Parlour, named for both the colour of its draperies and the carvings and plasterwork. It was one of her favourite parlours for entertaining: small enough that it didn't need a score of people in it to make it seem cosy, but large enough that the maid who scurried after them for propriety's sake could take a seat on the other side of the room where she could not overhear their conversation.

"You have been hard at work, I see," Lord Hamner said, as she put her lists to one side and invited him to sit. While they waited for privacy, she told him about her preparations for the charity events, and the complications of not yet knowing the venue for the auction.

"Mother has been saying the same thing," Lord Hamner said, "but she is most impressed with your gift for organisation, Miss Grenford."

Matilda blushed. "The credit goes to my guardian, my lord. Aunt Eleanor has seen me well trained."

A footman and two more maids carried in refreshments: tea, coffee, finely cut bread spread with cucumber relish, some of Monsieur Fournier's little iced cakes, date scones served with cream.

Lord Hamner surveyed it all with delight. "This is a feast, Miss Grenford."

She invited him to serve himself, while she fixed him the coffee that he asked for. As he filled his plate, he asked, "If we are not to stand on ceremony, I wonder if I might beg you to call me Hamner. Or even, should you wish it, Charles."

Matilda paused, his cup in her hand, then gathered her scattered wits and passed it to him. "You are very kind, Lo– Hamner."

He shook his head. "Not kind at all. You called me pompous, Matilda. You had the right of it, but I am trying to amend. May I call you Matilda?"

Matilda cast a glance at the maid, but she had her head bent low over her mending and was did not appear to be taking any notice of them.

"Just when we are alone," Hamner cajoled. "Or am I being an idiot again? I thought… I hoped that you might be coming to care for me as I do for you."

"I had no idea." Matilda lifted her chin, her lips firming as she remembered last year's tears. "Have we not travelled this path once before, my lord? You made your opinion of me clear at that time, did you not?"

His clear blue eyes met hers. If she did not guard her heart, he would break it all over again, but he sounded sincere. "I was a fool, and worse than a fool. A pompous prig, you said, and that hurt, because you were right."

"You kissed me, then spurned me and proposed to another woman," she reminded him.

"Ah." The colour rose in his face and he looked down at the coffee cup, dwarfed by his large capable hands. "You are Lady Felicity's friend. Of course, you know about that."

"What? You hoped to deceive me?"

"Not that!" The cup clattered as his hands shook, and he put it down on the side table. "I hoped I could explain it before you knew what an ass I had been. To burn for one woman and propose to another, as if they were interchangeable? My mother tells me I deserve for you to send me away and never speak to me again, but I hope to convince you that I have learned from my stupidity."

Almost without her volition, Matilda's head shook, slowly, more in disbelief than negation. "You despise the circumstances of my birth. You do not believe I would reflect credit to your name. Your words, Lord Hamner."

Hamner leaned forward as if he would grasp her hands, but stopped short of reaching for them. His voice vibrated with passion. "Do I regret that your birth has barred you from all the respect you deserve? Yes. You are the daughter of a duke, raised by a duchess, and a lady of uncommon intelligence, grace, and ability. You act always with propriety and dignity. You should take precedence with others of your rank, and I am indignant that you cannot. You would grace the name of the highest in the land. I was an ignorant fool to think otherwise, and an uncouth lout to say what I did. Though I hope my *actual* words were kinder, Matilda."

"Perhaps." She pursed her lips. "However, you agree that I took your meaning. As an apology for that kiss—I was humiliated, Charles, and I do not see how you expect me to forget it."

She only realized that she had slipped into calling him by his given name when his eyes lit up, but he did not capitalize on the error. "Not forget. But may I hope for forgiveness? In time? Give me leave to prove my sincerity by my devotion? I mean marriage, Matilda, in case you are in doubt. Yesterday, I saw you in danger, and I knew I could not be happy without you. I spoke to your brother, but he said some of what you have said, and told me that I would need to make my own petition to you. The choice of whether I am permitted to be your friend and your suitor is entirely yours."

"I do not know how to answer you." Hamner opened his mouth again, but Matilda held up her hand. "Enough. Lord Hamner, I shall think on what you have said, but we shall not speak of it again today. Aunt Eleanor appreciated your mother's help yesterday. Is she well?"

Hamner accepted her lead and they chatted for a few minutes about the work that Lady Hamner and Matilda had been doing together, and other matters to do with the Society.

"You said you had some news for my sister," Matilda said, after they had exhausted that subject. "Is it something you could entrust to me?"

"Good news, I hope. It was something the Earl of Hythe said to me a week or so ago, about a widow of a friend who was missing. I called on him this morning, and he confirmed that his widow is also Miss Jessica's. Not only can he attest to Lady Amhurst's marriage, he is the friend who sent her to her marriage, and Lord Amhurst appointed him as one of the guardians to the little boy. Once Miss Jessica's friend surfaces again, he will be happy to protect her and her child. Meanwhile, he intends to visit both her family and her husband's, and to start proceedings to have little Lord Amhurst declared his father's heir."

Matilda had not expected that. Jessica would be thrilled. "We owe you thanks again," she told Lord Hamner, and then, because he deserved a reward, "Charles."

9

Two days of fine weather were followed by snow, and Aldridge didn't return home. Every lady of the Society was now hard at work preparing for the third of February. They had commissioned three reprintings of Lady Georgiana's leaflets about the plight of returned soldiers and sailors, and of the widows and orphans of those who hadn't returned. The Frost Fair was looking more and more likely, and Matilda and Lady Hamner had created and distributed detailed instructions for those who had volunteered furniture, carpets, drapery, braziers, and other equipment for the ice.

Those creating bunting to decorate the venue had doubled their production so that both Haverford House and the space at on the ice would be draped in the Union Flag and the flags of the four kingdoms, regimental banners, and patriotic colours.

The three ladies in charge of organising ticket sales (ten pounds for the auction and Venetian Breakfast, and fifteen pounds for the ball) had a minor panic when they discovered that the Society's enthusiastic volunteers had promised more tickets than had been printed, but a quick meeting with the main committee resolved that both venues could find room for another fifty people.

Matilda and Jessica added acting as messenger for the duchess on top of their other duties. Charles—her rebel mind had fallen on the name, and it was a struggle to remember to call him by the more formal 'Hamner'—Charles was a loyal escort, willing to take them wherever they wished at a moment's notice. He did not speak again of courting Matilda, but now and then she caught him regarding her with wistful hunger.

And he continued to call her by her given name.

On Monday the thirty-first, the Thames was a complete field of ice from London Bridge to Blackfriars Bridge. The watermen, who had been barred from their usual profession for most of the month by the dangerous ice floes, quickly organised to test and then to control access to the ice. When Matilda went down to view the area she and Lady Hamner had chosen for the Haverford marquee, they demanded payment for helping her and her party over the small rivulet that had formed at the bank.

"That is outrageous," complained Charles, at her elbow as had become usual.

"Na, jes' think about it," the waterman coaxed. Matilda focused to translate his thick accent into words she could understand. "People pay us to take them on the river. Doesn't matter whether it is wet or dry. We did the same twenty odd years back, and before that, I reckon."

"Were you here for the last Frost Fair," Matilda asked? He certainly looked bent and wrinkled enough, what she could see of him in his greatcoat, cap, and scarf.

"That I were, me lady. And this bids fair to be a better one, it does."

Charles paid the couple of sixpences the man demanded, and then Matilda pointed out that he had now received the value of a boat ride. "Would you escort us, and tell us about the last Frost Fair, and what you expect for this one?"

They spent half an hour listening to the waterman's stories while they looked for a good site for the marquee and its subordi-nate tents—far enough from the main booths and activities of the fair that access was easy to control, and yet close enough that the ticket-holders could stroll the fair at their pleasure.

"That was clever," Charles noted, as they settled themselves back under the furs in his sleigh. "You've convinced the watermen to keep that part of the ice clear, and have negotiated a fee to make entry to the ice free to anyone who shows a ticket."

Matilda was pleased, too. "They shall do very well out of it: a lump sum deposit before the event and another afterwards, and all they have to do is keep our space clear, let our servants onto the ice to set up, and pass people who show a ticket on the third of February. Not that I grudge them. Imagine being unable to earn a living because the river you depend on freezes solid."

"You are a remarkable woman, Matilda Grenford," Charles said. Matilda tucked the comment away as she had the other compliments with which he lavished her. She had no doubt that he meant them, but she was still unsure about his change of heart.

Surely a man could not truly change such deep-seated opinions? He confessed himself that he was driven by desire. "To burn for one woman and propose to another," he said. Did desire last? If she married him, would he regret it? Would she?

She set her yearnings and her doubts to one side. The coming charity events were more than enough to think about, let alone keeping the duchess's injury (and its cause) from the world, and preventing Jessica from personally searching every gentlewomen's boarding house in London.

The sleigh passed the gates at Haverford House, the gatekeepers already familiar with it after several days of Hamner using it and the sturdy horses that drew it to squire Matilda around town.

Another, far more ornate sleigh, this one with a covered body and a team of three, stood at the steps. "Aldridge!" Matilda exclaimed, recognising the troika that her brother, Lord Jonathan Grenford, had sent to the duchess one Christmas when he was in Russia. Sure enough, the marquis was getting out from the equipage, tossing a laughing remark to his secretary, who emerged behind him.

As Charles brought their sleigh to a halt behind the Haverford troika, the marquis strolled along to greet them. "Matilda! And Lord Hamner, too." He handed Matilda from the carriage, and accepted the kiss she pressed to his cheek. "I am glad to see you home, Aldridge. You have made exceptional time!"

He gave the hand he had retained in his own a quick squeeze. "I could not miss the Society's auction and ball, Tilda. You shall have it on the ice as you hoped, I think."

"Yes. In fact," she waved a hand to include Charles in the discussion, "we have just come from there. All is arranged. I was about to bring Ch– Hamner inside to warm up with a mulled cider. Would you care to join us, Aldridge? Mr. Markinson, too, of course."

The secretary demurred, and trudged off to the heir's wing with a large case of papers, followed by a servant carrying the marquis's trunk, but Aldridge following Matilda into the main house.

"Your suit prospers, then, Hamner?" Matilda heard him ask.

"She has at least permitted me to assist her with the Society's event, my lord," Charles replied. Something in his voice hinted that, if she turned, she would find him keeping a wary eye on her. It comforted her to know the uncertainty was not all on one side.

When Matilda asked a footman to order refreshments to the family parlour, she was told that the duchess and her sisters were already there. Her Grace had emerged from seclusion while Matilda was out, the swelling on her face barely noticeable, the discolouration concealed with powder. She greeted Aldridge with pleasure, and gave Charles her hand to kiss.

"Matilda, Jessica has just been showing your excellent work to Frances and me. I am very proud of you, my dear. Hamner, I believe you have been a stalwart support these past few days. I thank you, and the Society will be grateful."

Frances, at almost thirteen the youngest Grenford ward, was cajoling Aldridge to take her for a ride in his sleigh. "Lord Hamner took us to Hyde Park skating, but his sleigh is very small, so we had to walk. Can we not take the troika, Aldridge? Tomorrow?"

"Perhaps, kitten," Aldridge told her, trying not to smile. "If I can make the time, where would you like to go?"

"The Frost Fair, of course." She was bouncing with excitement, and full of stories told to her by her governess and the servants about the Frost Fair of 1795.

Aldridge amused them for a while with his own memories. He must have been a boy of fifteen, and the stories he trotted out for

Frances were probably much sanitised. Before Matilda quite knew how it happened, Charles had not only been invited to go along on the expedition to the ice the next day, but was staying for a light meal. Somehow, without Matilda making any decisions about his place in her life, he had been accepted into their family circle.

In the end it was Charles, summoned by a message from Aldridge who could not, after all, avoid his ducal responsibilities, who took the three sisters down to the ice in the troika. If she had not already been in love with Charles, seeing his gentle way with Frances might have won her. The granite earl had gone as if he'd never been, leaving the charming, kind, courteous lord who had set stars in her eyes when he danced with her at her first ball.

He patiently took Frances off to see the elephant and have her fortune told while Matilda and Jessica took their turn answering questions at the Society's booth, making sure that every person attracted into the booth by Monsieur Fournier's delectable cakes and pastries left with at least one of Lady Georgiana's leaflets.

He insisted on paying for the four of them to have their caricatures drawn, first as individuals and then as a group, "to remember the day," he said.

He stopped a sputtering Lord Amhurst with a few stern words when the indignant man accosted them to demand to know which of them sent Lord Hythe to his doorstep with what the false earl called "a pack of damnable lies", and he sent Mr. Driscoll and a pack of his cronies scurrying away with a lift of an eyebrow and a glare that rivalled Aldridge at his most imperious.

By the time they made their way home, full of hawker food and beverages, the attendant footmen burdened with fairings, slightly silly with the experiences they'd tried and the sights they'd seen, first Frances and then Jessica had accepted Charles's invitation to call him by his first name. What could Matilda do but follow their example?

"What are your plans for tomorrow?" Charles asked. "May I be of service?"

"My duties for the auction and ball are all but over until the actual events," Matilda told him. "Tomorrow, Jessica and I will be preparing the food for our picnic baskets."

"With your own fair hands?" He smiled. "I shall be sure to take plenty of money with me to the auction." He intended to bid on her basket, then. Would he be impressed? In her spare time over the past week, she had consulted cook, visited Madame Fournier, who had once been the duchess's secretary and was now married to a famous chef, and pored over recipes.

Still, cooking skills—while favoured by the duchess—were not normally considered lady-like. Surely, he did not want a countess who cooked?

But he was telling Frances about trips with his mother and father to a cottage on their estate, where his father took him fishing and his mother made their meals. "Mother says that a lady should at least know the basics of every task she expects her servants to do, and I believe the same applies to a gentleman. I might not be able to get the shine on my boots that my valet manages, but if I travel alone, I am not completely helpless."

"That is what Aunt Eleanor says, too," Jessica told him.

They said goodbye to the earl and went upstairs to tell the duchess all about their afternoon. "Charles is very kind," Frances told her. "He said I might call him Charles. I think he wants to marry Matilda. I thought it might be Jessica, because the all men do want Jessica, but I am sure it is Matilda. He looks at her." Frances adopted an expression that could only be called languishing.

Matilda glared at Jessica, who could not speak for laughing. "Frances, such personal remarks are not appropriate."

Frances looked at Matilda then decided to address herself to Aunt Eleanor. "I only want to know, Aunt Eleanor," she explained. "If Matilda marries Charles, will I be the bride's attendant, like my cousin Daisy was when cousin Susan married?"

"If that is your hope, dear Frances," Aunt Eleanor replied, "you might begin by not annoying your sister."

10

Matilda, with a little help and advice from the cook, made pies and puddings, roasted several different kinds of meat. She added cut cheese and fresh fruit to the basket that already held crockery, cutlery, condiments, and several types of drink.

Tomorrow, after she made the bread, would make a salmagundi with cold chicken, hard-boiled eggs, anchovy fillets, beetroot, red cabbage, cooked tongue, celery, bright salad leaves, and cucumbers from the Haverford hot house.

Jessica teased that she was feeding an army, but she helped prepare the roasts, and would use some of the meat in her own basket. Jessica was also making gingerbread cake, pork pies, and syllabub.

They were in the thick of it when a message came down to say Lord Hamner had called. Matilda's impulse to cast down what she was doing and hurry to see him annoyed her almost as much as his arrogance in calling when she had told him she was busy.

"Please inform Lord Hamner that I am not 'at home'," she told the footman.

She glared at Jessica's grin, and Jessica, who had opened her mouth, changed her mind and turned back to the little shortbread biscuits that she was cutting out with a tin cutter shaped like a star.

It was Matilda's choice to refuse Charles, but she went to bed that night with aching with something that felt like homesickness. The day had not been complete without him.

Charles was up early on the morning of the Ladies' Society Venetian Breakfast. Aldridge had invited him to break his fast at Haverford House so he could offer to escort the young ladies to the ice to oversee the erection of the marquee and its attendant tents.

He walked the short distance to the mansion, since the ice made riding dangerous for both man and horse, treading carefully as he mulled over the words his mother had said the previous evening, as he daydreamed after dinner, imagining Matilda in the countess's chair and trying not to feel disconsolate at not seeing her for a whole day.

"When you propose to Miss Grenford, Charles—you do plan to propose, do you not?" She waited for his nod. "Tell her that I welcome her as a daughter-in-law. She worries about the circumstances of her birth, and she may need reassurance about my opinion."

"I do not care who her mother was," Charles began, indignantly, but his mother held up a hand to stop him.

"Nor I, and that is my point. I cannot imagine a match that would better please me. She will make a magnificent countess, but that is beside the point. She is good for you, and she loves you, and she will be a wonderful mother for the beautiful grandchildren the pair of you will make for me. I will be sure to tell her myself, but I cannot raise the issue with her until you have actually proposed."

"I am glad to have your blessing, Mother, but I would marry Matilda without it."

Mother laughed. "So I would hope."

It was too early to propose, was it not? She was starting to like him a little, but he could not fool himself that he'd won back the ground he'd lost at the house party just over a year ago.

Still, when he was admitted to the Haverford House family

breakfast room, he could have sworn her eyes lit up at the sight of him, and she readily accepted his escort in place of her brother. "I will bring Her Grace down in time for the auction," Aldridge promised.

The area the watermen had set aside for the event was humming with activity. The marquee was up already, with streams of servants bringing in furnishing, carpets, and drapes to turn it into a sumptuous reception room, with a stage at one end for the auctioneer.

Charles found himself in charge of managing the furbishment of a number of smaller tents among a dozen set up to provide dining areas for the successful bidders. For the next several hours, he went from task to task as directed by young ladies of the Society, each of whom marshalled one part of the preparation.

At last, they paused for a hot drink and a collective sigh of satisfaction. The patronesses and elder committee members were beginning to arrive. Soon, they would set up the reception lines for the ticket holders, and the event would begin. Charles made his way to Matilda's side.

"Nearly time," he commented.

"I am afraid no one will come," she confessed. "I know it is silly, but there you are."

"I think only those who are recluses or infirm will miss it," Charles assured her. This evidence of the insecurity she hid under her efficiency and competence set him yearning to hold her in his arms and protect her from every chill wind. "You have sold hundreds of tickets, and I expect them all to be here. Such an unusual setting! It was a brilliant idea to hold the event here, and the marquee and tents look marvellous. Very comfortable, too. You and my mother are largely to be credited with organising the venue, or so I understand."

Matilda blushed. "Your mother has worked very hard, and has come up with most of the good ideas."

"She says the same about you," Charles assured her. "She is most impressed with you, Matilda." Was this the time to pass on Mother's message, but no, they were being called to form the reception lines. And there were the first ticket-holders, queuing in the cold, dozens of them.

Even with three entry points, gatekeepers to check tickets, and three reception lines, it took more than half an hour to bring the bulk of the ticket holders inside; not just the usual supporters of the charity, but dozens, perhaps hundreds of the *beau monde* who would otherwise never put their hands in their pockets for the charitable cause in question.

Matilda, when she made her way back to Charles's side, suggested it was partly the potential for scandal in the nature of the auction. "Sale of a lady's time? Shocking!"

Jessica and Percy, who had joined them, laughed and declared, "But it is all for charity. Her Grace told Lady Jersey that the most proper of the ton's sticklers could have no objection to a lady offering food and the pleasure of her company in support of a good cause, and Countess Leuven agreed."

The duchess, any signs of her injury well concealed, opened the auction and introduced her friend, Brigadier General Lord Redepenning, known almost universally as Lord Henry. He explained how the auction would work, and in no time at all was knocking down baskets to the eager bidders.

It was fun to watch. Lord Henry had the crowd laughing with his quips, egging on the bidders, and cheering the winners. Some baskets went to acknowledged suitors and husbands. Even for those, the bidding was often fierce, and Percy Cummins' basket sold for the princely sum of one hundred pounds, the Earl of Trehallow outbidding everyone else, including Aldridge.

"Next," Lord Henry announced, "we have a basket packed by Miss Jessica Grenford." He lifted the lid, and made an artistic show of scenting the contents. "Gingerbread, ladies and gentlemen. And is this champagne? Much more, too. I cannot begin to describe the treats in store for the lucky winner."

The first bid of five pounds came from the other side of the room, and another followed, then another, until the bidding was up to ten pounds. Then Basil Driscoll put in a bid of fifteen pounds. Jessica looked around in alarm. Matilda cast a pleading look at

Charles. He waited for Aldridge to intervene, but the marquis had been called out of the marquee by one of the servants on duty.

Another bid, this one for seventeen pounds. It was a friend of Trehallow. She'd be safe with James Marr.

"Twenty pounds," Driscoll shouted.

Charles waited for another bid. Nothing. Matilda met his eyes again and, as Lord Henry raised his gavel, Charles answered the plea.

"Fifty pounds!" The basket was knocked down to him, and Jessica came to take his arm. "Come with me," Charles begged Matilda, and led both sisters to the front, where Jessica's basket awaited.

Matilda's basket was one of the last to be auctioned. Lord Henry had been warning the remaining men to bid high or be left out, and the dwindling crowd had responded with some ridiculous bids. A basket by Margaret Bellham, a spinster on her seventh season, sold for 90 pounds, but then she was known to employ a famous cook.

Miss Cratchett, heiress to a mill owner, and one of those maidens about whom people say, 'but she has a lovely personality' was escorted off to lunch by Lord Aldridge, beaming widely, though whether at the lunch companion she had gained or the seventy-five pounds contributed to the charity it was hard to say.

Hamner waited with Jessica and Matilda. When Lord Henry announced Matilda's basket, Charles felt her tense beside him.

"Ten pounds," shouted James Marr.

"Fifteen," countered Charles.

"I say," said Vernon Mellbarrow. "He already has a basket and a lovely lunch guest."

"Nothing in the rules to say he cannot buy another," Lord Henry ruled.

The Marquess of Welbrook bid twenty pounds, and James Marr topped him by another five.

"Thirty pounds." That was Driscoll, the evil swine.

Two of the bidders had their heads together. Mellbarrow shouted out one hundred pounds, adding, "It is unfair for Hamner to have two baskets. If the lady will accept both James and myself, we are happy to continue bidding. Seventy-five pounds!"

"One hundred pounds," said Charles, firmly, following the strategy displayed earlier by the Earl of Trehallow. In triumph, he collected his second basket of the afternoon, and marched off with the Grenford sisters, collecting his mother to play chaperone on his way out of the marquee.

11

One of the footmen led Matilda's party to a table in one of the larger tents, where a half a dozen groups already enjoyed their meal.

Mr. Marr and Mr. Mellbarrow arrived, escorting Cecilia Fournier, and boasting about winning a basket by the best chef in London. "In Europe, gentlemen, if you please," Cecilia scolded, laughing. She winked at Matilda as she and the gentlemen passed the table. "My husband would not argue if you said 'in the world'!" They took a table in the far corner, and a few moments later Monsieur Fournier himself joined them.

"There were many more bidders than baskets," Charles commented. "The rest will be satisfied with food from the hawkers, I suppose."

"Not at all," Matilda explained. "As soon as the auction is over, a feast will be spread in the marquee for all those ticket holders who have neither contributed nor purchased a basket. No one will go hungry." It would be a varied offering, too, for no one had made merely enough for one basket, and the surplus food had all been donated to serve as lunch for the disappointed.

Charles smiled at Matilda and then glanced around the table, to include his mother and Jessica in his comments. "The Society is to be congratulated. I can see that winter picnics with basket auctions is going to become the next thing for raising charitable funds.

"We shall have to put our thinking caps on for next year," Matilda told him. "Aunt Eleanor does not like to repeat herself."

Just then, they were interrupted. Mr. Driscoll must have purchased one of the last baskets. He and Lord Amhurst hurried into the tent with Miss Fairley, a timid wallflower who had only recently joined the Society and whose chaperone, a prune-faced old besom of an aunt, seemed determined to throw her at any gentleman who showed the least interest. Where was the woman? Surely, Matilda thought, she had not abandoned poor Miss Fairley to a reprobate like Driscoll?

"They are here," Driscoll said, and he plonked the basket he was carrying onto a spare table. He took a pace towards the table where the Grenford sisters sat with Charles and Lady Hamner, but stopped when Charles stood and met his eyes.

He turned back to Amhurst, saying in a loud voice, "I cannot believe we are expected to eat with such alley sweepings."

Charles, his fists clenched, took a step towards the horrid man, but Matilda put a hand on his arm and shook her head. "Pretend it is not about us," she murmured, keeping her voice low. "He wants to make a display. Ignoring him is the best strategy."

Lady Hamner smiled her approval. "Quite right, my dear. Take the moral high ground, I always say."

Jessica sighed. "So does Aunt Eleanor."

With some reluctance, Charles sank back into his seat and attempted to join in the renewed conversation, stopping frequently to glare at Amhurst and Driscoll. He was not the only one, as they continued to exchange remarks about the smell, contagion, and moral turpitude, pretending not to look at Matilda and Jessica, but making sure the entire tent knew who they were targeting with their attacks.

At the other tables, people glared or turned their backs, according to their natures. Matilda did her best not to look their way, but when she heard Miss Fairley sob, she could not help herself. A few yards away, the girl was attempting to shrink in her seat, face scarlet, and in tears. Before she thought about it, she was on her feet and marching over.

She completely ignored the two men, and held out her hand to Miss Fairley. "Will you join us, Miss Fairley? We have plenty."

Miss Fairley brightened and began to rise.

"We bought your time with your basket," Driscoll snapped, and Miss Fairley dropped back into her chair. "Go away, Miss Grenford." He sneered over the name, making it another insult. "A good girl like Miss Fairley doesn't keep company with the likes of you."

Charles had followed, and was at Matilda's shoulder. Mr. Marr and the Earl of Chadbourn approached, and so did a number of the other men in the tent.

Amhurst addressed the tent at large. "We are trying to eat our basket in peace. This woman, who should not be allowed in polite company, is causing trouble. Just like her sister did, taking the part of the trollop who tried to pass off her bastard as my nephew's son." Driscoll told him to be quiet, but he rounded on Jessica, his face in a snarl. "Where have you hidden her? I'll have the law on you. I'll ruin you, and your sisters."

Charles, Marr, and another man had him in a hold, and were dragging him towards the entrance to the tent, Driscoll having stepped aside with his hands spread. He continued to shout, "I'll have you drummed out of London. You'll be selling yourself in the streets by the time I'm done with you, you bitch!"

Before they reached the heavy drape that kept the cold air from inside, it lifted, and the Lords Hythe and Sutton stepped through, followed by Hythe's sisters, Lady Felicity and Lady Sutton.

"May we take Marbeck off your hands?" Hythe asked Charles. "He has some questions to answer about his treatment of the true Earl of Amhurst and the child's mother."

"I am the true Earl of Amhurst, you fools, and the bitch that chased after that useless brat Samuel has undoubtedly frozen to death and her whelp with her." Amhurst screamed.

"On the contrary," Hythe told him, "Lady Amhurst and the earl are safe and well."

Felicity and Sophia skirted the men and crossed to where Jessica and Matilda stood, their eyes wide. "Her letter finally reached

Hythe," Felicity explained. "He has all the proof she needs to put Mr. Marbeck back into the hole where he belongs, and she is now staying with my sister and Sutton at the Winshire mansion."

Driscoll had started shouting now. The whole tent—perhaps half the fair—heard him break with his former bosom bow. "You lied to me. You told me the woman was deranged and she didn't even know your nephew." The false earl was led away, with Driscoll following.

"I'll see my sister's marriage declared void, Amhurst," he was shouting. "No, you aren't Amhurst are you, Marbeck? You promised to make her wealthy and a countess and now you are nothing and I'm not going to let you drag her down with you!"

Matilda, managing to keep her voice level and calm, invited the Belvoir sisters to join her table, "and you, Miss Fairley, if you care to do so."

Several people helped them push tables together, and soon they made a merry party, putting the unpleasantness behind them, but interrupted every few minutes as one after another of the other diners came over to the table to ask after Miss Fairley's wellbeing or just to show their support with a friendly comment. Matilda was touched. Ever since she and Jessica had attracted the attention of bullies at school, she expected to be shunned when her origins were discussed. Not so, it seemed. This group, at least, accepted her despite those vile men.

After the discouraging start, they had a delightful lunch, and even Miss Fairley came out of her shell enough to talk about the gown she planned to wear at the ball that night, and to shyly agree to dances with several of the gentlemen.

Before she knew where the time had gone, Matilda was climbing back into the troika for the return journey to Haverford House. She parted with the Hamners at the banks of the Thames, but not before Charles had asked for a private word with her this evening before dinner. He was going to propose. She just knew it. What she didn't know was what she was going to reply.

Haverford House seethed like a stirred ants' nest, servants hurrying in every direction as they made the final preparations for the duchess's grand dinner followed by the charity ball. Charles followed the footman sent to conduct him through the ordered chaos to a private parlour in the family wing.

He had dressed with enormous care, driving his valet demented by changing his mind three times about his waistcoat, rejecting six cravats before settling on the seventh, and hesitating for twenty minutes on his choice of fobs. The valet would probably slit his wrists in despair if he could see how Charles had set his hair in disarray by running his fingers through it, and ruined the hard-won perfection of the cravat by tugging it further open because he felt it choking him.

Then the door opened. Matilda entered the room and he lost his breath again. She was magnificent in a violet gown that hugged her curves before sweeping out into a deceptively simple skirt that avoided fashionable ruffles in favour of more subtle stitching that added detail without fuss. The neckline was low enough to rivet his attention while still high enough to be demure by the current standards. She wore pearls at her neck, her wrists, dangling from her ears and glowing in her dark hair, and the blue eyes he met when he wrenched his attention from the snowy skin displayed by her décolletage had taken on a violet cast from the gown.

He gazed, losing track of time and space, until she said his name. "Charles?"

"I had a speech." His voice croaked, and he swallowed. "I do not remember a word."

With one hand, index finger outstretched, he traced an inch or so away from her face. "Why did I try so hard to resist you, you beautiful woman?"

It was the wrong thing to say. Her nostrils flared. "Because I am the base-born daughter of a harlot."

"I cannot remember why I thought that important," he confessed. "You are the beloved sister of the next Duke of Haverford, the ward of the current duchess, and a lady of impeccable education, training and manners. That is not why I love you, though."

Her eyes softened. "You love me?"

"That was part of the speech. It is the only bit I remember. I look into your eyes, and I forget my own name."

"Why?" Matilda asked.

"Why do I forget? No? Why now?" She coloured, and he realized what she was asking. "Why do I love you? How can I explain something that has grown in my heart without my knowledge, even against my will?" He took both of her hands, and suddenly the words began to flow.

"I have been attracted to you since the first time we danced, but that is desire, and desire is a part of love but not the whole. I do desire you, my love, more and more each day, but I also admire you, I like being with you, I enjoy talking to you, I respect you. I want to see you every morning when I wake, to spend my days with you, to have the right to dance the first waltz with you at every ball, and to go home with you every night. I want to see your belly rounded with our child, and watch you as you gently teach them the way I've seen you teach your little sister. I want you and only you as my countess and the mother of my children. I want to grow old with you, Matilda Grenford."

He dropped to one knee. "Miss Grenford, I esteem you with all my heart. Will you do me the very great honour of becoming my wife?"

He waited, his anxiety rising as she said nothing, despair taking over as tears rose and began to leak from her pansy eyes. Then she began to nod as she slipped to her own knees and reached out for him. "Yes. Oh, yes. Charles, I love you, too."

For more than a year, Charles had kept to himself the fact that the Haverford Ice Princess kissed like a flame. As he abandoned his own granite facade for once and for all, he rejoiced in her heat. This time was even better than the last, and the best was yet to come. Though perhaps not here in a family parlour where her brother or sisters could walk in at any time.

"I hope you do not want a long betrothal," he whispered, between kisses.

She broke off her attempt to completely unravel his cravat. "Not long," she agreed.

Her fervent answer demanded that he kiss her again, losing himself so deep he didn't know they were no longer alone until a voice behind him said, "I trust you are betrothed to my sister, Hamner, for it would be most inconvenient to start the evening's celebrations by killing you."

Matilda leapt to her feet, blushing, and Charles rose more slowly, to put a defiant arm around her waist. She leaned into his side.

"Do not tease the poor man," said the duchess. "Of course, he and Matilda are betrothed, and I am delighted, my dears, for I could tell you were made for one another."

Mother was there, too, declaring her own pleasure at the match, and Jessica and Frances were hugging their sister.

Charles tidied his cravat and his hair while Aldridge ordered champagne and talked about announcing the betrothal at the dinner in less than an hour. Mother had arrived early, but soon the other guests would be gathering.

Perhaps Charles had made a tactical error, asking for her hand before a dinner that would mean two hours of propriety in the company of others. And then the ball, another five hours, though at least then he'd have opportunities to touch her, to murmur endearments, perhaps to steal a kiss.

Matilda emerged from the tidying hands of her sisters and their eyes met in a long warm embrace. It was enough to soothe his impatience. Perhaps the duchess would rearrange her table so Matilda and her new betrothed could walk in together and sit side by side. And if not, he could be patient. He would have a lifetime to find countless ways of melting Matilda.

THE END

This novella is part of the series *The Return of the Mountain King*. It is set a few months after the end of the second novel, *To Mend the Broken Hearted*. The first, *To Wed a Proper Lady*, tells the story of Jamie Winderfield, who has been ordered to find a proper English bride, but can't persuade Sophia Belvoir, the one he has fallen in love with, that he is serious about her.

The next novel in the series is *To Claim the Long-Lost Lover*, which will be out some time in July.

Read on for **more about the Mountain King series**.

For a free short story every two months, subscribe to Jude's newsletter on http://judeknightauthor.com/newsletter/

ENJOY THESE BOOKS BY JUDE KNIGHT

Regency books

The Return of the Mountain King series

James Winderfield, exiled third son of the Duke of Winshire, is back to inherit the ducal title.

In 1812, high Society is rocked by the return of the Earl of Sutton, heir to the dying Duke of Winshire. James Winderfield, Earl of Sutton, Winshire's third and only surviving son, has long been thought dead, but his reappearance is not nearly such a shock as those he brings with him, the children of his deceased Persian-born wife and fierce armed retainers, both men and women.

The Duke of Haverford, his one-time rival in love, sets out to destroy him, and his children with him, but Sutton is no longer the friendless, open-hearted youth that was exiled for his temerity. Even inheriting his father's title won't stop his enemies from trying to kill him. But no one, his people whisper, ever wins against the King of the Mountains.

As the new Duke of Winshire's four older children and his twin nieces navigate society to find acceptance and a love of their own, Winshire rekindles his acquaintance with the influential and beloved matriarch, Eleanor, Duchess of Haverford. Their time is long past; their friendship, though, is golden.

Paradise Regained (prequel novella)

James yearns to end a long journey in the arms of his loving family. But his father's agents offer the exiled prodigal forgiveness and a place in Society — if he abandons his foreign-born wife and children to return to England.

With her husband away, Mahzad faces revolt, invasion and betrayal in the mountain kingdom they built together. A queen without her king, she will not allow their dream and their family to be destroyed.

To Wed a Proper Lady — The Barbarian and the Bluestocking (novel 1 in the series)

Everyone knows James needs a bride with impeccable blood lines. He needs Sophia's love more.

James, eldest son of the Earl of Sutton, must marry to please his grandfather, the Duke of Winshire, and to win social acceptance for himself and his father's other foreign-born children. But only Lady Sophia Belvoir makes his heart sing, and to win her, he must invite himself to spend Christmas at the home of his father's greatest enemy: the man who is fighting in Parliament to have his father's marriage declared invalid and the Winderfield children made bastards.

Sophia keeps secret her *tendre* for James, Lord Elfingham. After all, the whole of Society knows he is pursuing the younger Belvoir sister, not the older one left on the shelf after two failed betrothals. Even when he asks for her hand in marriage, she still can't quite believe that he loves her.

(This book was first published as a novella, and has been extensively rewritten to make it a novel. The novella was in the Bluestocking Belles' collection *Holly and Hopeful Hearts*.)

<u>*A Suitable Husband*</u>

A chef from the slums, however talented, is no fit mate for the cousin of a duke, however distant. But Cedrica Grenford can dream. (novella)

To Mend the Broken-Hearted — The Healer and the Hermit (novel 2 in the series)

Trained as a healer, Ruth Winderfield is happiest in a sickroom. When she's caught up in a smallpox epidemic and finds herself quarantined at the remote manor of a reclusive lord, the last thing she expects is to find her heart's desire. A pity he does not feel the same. She must return to London's ballrooms, where the wealth of her family and the question over her birth make her a target for the unscrupulous and a pariah to the high-sticklers.

Valentine, Earl of Ashbury, is horrified when an impertinent bossy female turns up with several sick children, including the two girls he is responsible for. He hasn't seen his niece and his daughter—if she is his daughter—since his faithless wife and treacherous brother died three years ago. He reluctantly gives them shelter. Even more reluctantly, he helps with the nursing.

When Ruth goes, she takes his heart with him. When jealous relatives lie about their time together, Val must face his past and win her back, not just for himself, but for the children he has come to love.

Melting Matilda (This book)

Sparks flew a year ago when the Granite Earl kissed the Ice Princess under the mistletoe. Matilda Grenford is a lady and the ward of a duchess, but the daughter of a famous courtesan. Charles, Earl of Hamner, seeks a countess of impeccable bloodlines, not one whose scandalous birth would offend every noble ancestor back to the Norman Conquest. But neither of them can forget that kiss.

Coming at two-monthly intervals from July 2021

To Tame the Wild Rake — The Sinner and the Saint

The Marquis of Aldridge doesn't want to yearn for the sister of a friend from his raking days. Especially since she has rejected him in no uncertain terms. Charlotte Winderfield, niece of the Mountain King, keeps a secret that bars her from marriage, but even if she found the courage to trust, she would never trust a rake.

To Claim the Long-Lost Lover — The Diamond and the Doctor

Her girlhood lover is back, as compelling as ever, but Sarah Winderfield, Charlotte's twin, cannot forget he abandoned her, leaving her to face the anger of her family and worse. Sarah is even lovelier than when she was a girl, but Miles Pointon has not forgiven her for betraying him to her father's revenge: indenture to the Caribbean and years of servitude.

The Golden Redepennings series

True love is rare and elusive, but they won't settle for less.

<u>*Candle's Christmas Chair*</u> (A novella in *The Golden Redepennings* series)

They are separated by social standing and malicious lies. He has until Christmas to convince her to give their love another chance.

<u>*Gingerbread Bride*</u> (A novella in *The Golden Redepennings* series)

Mary runs from an unwanted marriage and finds adventure, danger and her girlhood hero, coming once more to her rescue.

<u>*Farewell to Kindness*</u> (Book 1 in *The Golden Redepennings* series)

Love is not always convenient. Anne and Rede have different goals, but when their enemies join forces, so must they.

<u>*A Raging Madness*</u> (Book 2 in *The Golden Redepennings* series)

Their marriage is a fiction. Their enemies are all too real. Uncovering the truth will need all the trust Ella and Alex can find.

<u>*The Realm of Silence*</u> (Book 3 in *The Golden Redepennings* series)

Rescue her daughter, destroy her dragons, defeat his demons, return to his lonely life. How hard can it be?

Unkept Promises (Book 4 in *The Golden Redepennings* series)

Mia hopes to negotiate a comfortable marriage. Jules wants his wife to return to England, where she belongs. Love confounds them both.

Other Regency books

A Baron for Becky

She was a fallen woman. How could the men who loved her help set her back on her feet?

House of Thorns

His rose thief bride comes with a scandal that threatens to tear them apart.

Lord Calne's Christmas Ruby

One wealthy merchant's heiress with an aversion to fortune hunters. One an impoverished earl with a twisted hand. Combine and stir with one villainous rector. (novella)

Revealed in Mist

As spy and enquiry agent, Prue and David worked to uncover secrets, while hiding a few of their own.

The Beast Next Door (A novella in the Bluestocking Belles collection _Valentines from Bath_)

In all the assemblies and parties, no-one Charis met could ever match the beast next door.

Lunch-length reads: story collections

Hand-Turned Tales and _Lost in the Tale_

A double handful of short stories and novellas. _Hand-Turned Tales_ is free from most eretailers. Try the range of Jude's imagination one bite at a time, in a lunch-length read.

If Mistletoe Could Tell Tales

A repackaging of six published Christmas stories: four novellas and two novelettes. Because nothing enhances the magic of Christmas like the magic of love.

Hearts in the Land of Ferns

Five stories all set in New Zealand: two historical and three contemporary suspense. All That Glisters has been published in Hand-Turned Tales. The other four have all been published in multi-author collections, but never before in a collection of Jude Knight stories.

ABOUT JUDE KNIGHT

I've been trying to be a novelist since I was fourteen. I was a good enough reader to see that the first two attempts (one when I was fourteen and one in my early twenties) weren't good enough to publish. Then along came life. A seriously ill child who required years of therapy; a rising mortgage that led to a full-time job; my own chronic illness… the writing took a back seat.

As the years passed, the fear grew. I'd waited so long. If I never finished any of the dozens of novels I started, no one would ever judge them.

My mother believed in me, and on the way home from that great lady's funeral, I realised I'd left it too late for Mum to ever hold a print copy of one of my fiction books. So I replaced the fear of finishing with the fear of not finishing, by telling everyone I knew that I was writing a novel.

In the years since I published my first fiction book just before Christmas in 2014, I published seven novels, thirteen novellas, a heap of shorter stories, and more novellas in group anthologies. I plan to keep going till I run out of years.

I write historical fiction with a large helping of romance, a splash of Regency, and a twist of suspense.

I then try to figure out how to slot it into a genre category.

I'm mad keen on history, enjoy what happens to people in the crucible of a passionate relationship, and love to use a good mystery and some real danger as mechanisms to torture my characters.

In my other identity as Judy Knighton, I've been a plain language consultant specialising in contracts, insurance policies, and financial disclosure statements. Fiction is more fun.

Website and blog: http://judeknightauthor.com/
Book blurbs and links: http://judeknightauthor.com/books/

Do you like news before anyone else, plus discounts, and free stuff?

Sign up to my newsletter. The main newsletter goes out once every two months, and includes news about coming books, discounts, contests, and events. Every newsletter also has news about books from my author friends, and a free story that I write just for newsletter subscribers.

In between newsletters, if I have something exciting to share I occasionally sends a one-topic email.

Free book as a thank you

As a thank you for subscribing to my newsletter, you can expect a series of three emails, the first offering a free copy of one of my books, and the next two with links to other free stories. So why not subscribe today?

Subscribe to newsletter: http://judeknightauthor.com/newsletter/